IN THE BEGINNING, before the creation of the World, there was only the Great Being Rujir-Zakurele. Rujir-Zakurele was everything and all there was. But since there was only Rujir-Zakurele, the Great Being was bored and fell asleep. As Rujir-Zakurele fell asleep, the Great Being began to dream.

As Rujir-Zakurele dreamed, the World was created.

Consequently, the World was created on accident and without any manner of plan or purpose. As the Great Being dreamed, the World amassed like a great tree, sprouting off countless branches, which sprouted off further branches, entangling and enmeshing with one another. Branches of the World decayed and fell away, but the branches that had sprouted off from them kept growing and sprouting off further branches, such that the World moved like a great snake chasing after its tail, but continuing to shed its skin and grow at such an expansive rate that it was never able to reach the end of itself.

Within this dreamed World, entities known as humans came to develop complex consciousnesses and societies, and some of their stories came to develop plots—as if they actually had some kind of meaning.

In this way, the World developed, diversified, and expanded in ways entirely out of the control of Rujir-Zakurele, who was very tired of everything and yet could not wake up from it.

Tales from the
Mythusian Empire
books can be read in
any order.

SAND TO GLASS
Copyright © 2021 by Remy Apepp.
Cover design by Nada Orlic.

Thinklings Books
1400 Lloyd Rd. #552
Wickliffe, OH 44092
thinklingsbooks.com

SAND

TO

GLASS

by

Remy Apepp

Thinklings Books, LLC
Wickliffe, OH

The Royal Family of Ordyuk

King & High Priest: **Agamenjiyr Nji Madubabakar**
/AG-uh-MEN-jeer   nuh-JEE   MAD-
oo-BAB-uh-KAR/

Queen & High Priestess: **Ythiris Rida Madubabakar**
/ih-THEER-iss   REE-duh/

Crown Prince: **Diyomendon Tdroki
Madubabakar**
/DEE-oh-MEN-dawn
tuh-duh-ROW-kee/

Princess: **Naliki Rkalla Madubabakar**
/NAL-ih-kee   arr-KAL-uh/

Second Prince: **Luxanthus Nkidu Madubabakar**
/lux-AN-thus   en-KEE-doo/

Third Prince: **Rezekyrios Tmra Madubabakar**
/reh-zuh-KEER-ee-OSE
TOOM-ruh/

The Visitors

Mysterious traveler: **Aodhealbhach Sinngan**
/ey-awd-HEEL-bach SIN-gan/

The King of Mythus: **Morphioce**
/MORE-fee-OSE/

THE RELEVANT DEITIES

(Singular = Daimu; Plural = Daimmu)

Fire: **Ingaru**
/in-GAR-oo/

Death: **Injal**
/EEN-jal/

Matters of Blood: **Ishanu**
(Family, Passion, Revenge, Sacrifice, /ee-SHAW-noo/
Violence, War)

Chaos: **Jajul**
/ja-JOOL/

Music and Dancing: **Kulele**
/koo-LEL/

Sky, Storms, Wind, Air, Rain: **Nimuru**
/nih-MER-oo/

Order: **Rujir**
/roo-JEER/

Beasts: **Silbalmu**
/sil-BALL-moo/

Dreams: **Zakurele**
/za-kur-EL/

SAND TO GLASS

I

DIYOMENDON TDROKI MADUBABAKAR, first son of King Agamenjiyr and Queen Ythiris, was the Crown Prince of the Desert Kingdom of Ordyuk.

He hated it.

He was the one who would be inheriting the throne, and the expectations for the kingdom's future were riding on him. He was supposed to be perfect. He was supposed to be the best. He wasn't allowed to make mistakes. He wasn't allowed to do anything that could get him injured. His life was too vital. Everyone bowed down to him and did things for him. He wasn't allowed to do those things for himself.

He was supposed to be happy. He wasn't supposed to be bitter or angry. He was supposed to glory in being the heir. He was supposed to like having the power to tell everyone what to do and not to have to do anything for himself. He was supposed to feel honored and superior because of it.

He didn't. All he felt was frustrated, constrained, suffocated, and angry beyond belief.

Diyomendon Tdroki was the Crown Prince of the Kingdom of Ordyuk, and he hated the role with a burning, fiery passion.

NALIKI RKALLA MADUBABAKAR, second child and only daughter of King Agamenjiyr and Queen Ythiris, was the sole Princess of the Desert Kingdom of Ordyuk.

She loved it.

Everybody waited on her. She got whatever she wanted. She got away with whatever she wanted. She was being groomed to eventually marry an important member of the government or military. The idea was for her to grow up feeling beautiful and to develop an agreeable personality, so everyone was sweet to her. She was spoiled, really. It was great.

Her brothers had it a lot harder. She felt bad for them, sometimes. Other times she enjoyed messing with them, because they couldn't do anything to her. She did love them, though.

She was very glad, however, that she'd been born a girl and not a boy.

LUXANTHUS NKIDU MADUBABAKAR, third child of King Agamenjiyr and Queen Ythiris, was the Second Prince of the Desert Kingdom of Ordyuk.

He didn't really think about it.

His status and role as the second prince were a fact of his life, and he accepted it. It made sense that the crown prince should focus on academics and the technicalities of running a kingdom, while being forbidden from intense physical training that could cause him grievous injury, and it made sense that he himself as the second prince could forego most of the intellectual training and focus on the physical, so someday he could become the kingdom's trusted warrior and war general. Since he wasn't going to become king, he was far more expendable and could afford to get injured and be pushed to his physical limits. Because of that, it also made sense that he must bear the burden of the punishments for his older brother's mistakes.

It didn't bother him any. It made sense. And he was good at what he did. When it came to physical feats, he was naturally gifted. Far more so than either his older or his younger brother. The brunt of physical burdens therefore should fall onto him.

He didn't resent either of his brothers for any of it.

REZEKYRIOS TMRA MADUBABAKAR, fourth child of King Agamenjiyr and Queen Ythiris, was the Third Prince of the Desert Kingdom of Ordyuk.

He was always thinking about it.

The crown prince, princess, and second prince had been born for strategic purposes, each of them about a year apart. Rezekyrios Tmra had been born seven years after the second prince, nine years after the first. His birth had not been for any strategic purpose. King Agamenjiyr and Queen Ythiris—although their marriage had had its strategic purposes—deeply loved each other, and Rezekyrios Tmra had simply been the product of a night of passion.

His parents and his older siblings loved him, but he felt lost and inadequate. In regard to the kingdom, he did not have a clear role, and he wasn't particularly good at anything. In academics, he was subpar; and when it came to anything physical, he had two left feet. He was fully capable of tripping on his own toes when he ran and giving himself black eyes with his own hands when he flailed.

He loved his family, but he didn't know how he fit in it or what worth he had.

YTHIRIS RIDA MADUBABAKAR, Queen of Ordyuk, considered them her Gem Children.

Her dear Tdroki, with his fiery red-orange eyes like carnelians and his hair that stuck up like flame and couldn't be tamed; her dear Rkalla, with her deep red eyes like garnets and her straight hair that she wore down to her shoulders, with her bangs pulled out of her face and braided around her head like a circlet; her dear Nkidu, with his eyes like gold and his hair that fell down in smooth, effortless waves even though he never brushed it; her dear Tmra, with his eyes of two different colors, his right eye black like obsidian and his left a light yellow-orange like amber, and his hair that fell partially down and stuck partially up in obstinate cowlicks until her daughter one day braided them with metal wire and weighted them down with gold and obsidian beads.

What they shared was their warm bronze skin-tone, partway between her slightly lighter tone and her husband's slightly darker one. Both Tdroki and Nkidu shared their father's deep, multi-toned brown hair that shifted shades in the light, while Rkalla and Tmra shared Ythiris's darker, more single-toned shade.

Their particular idiosyncrasies suited them, Ythiris thought. Tdroki with his fiery personality, Rkalla with her passionate one, Nkidu with his effortless talent, and Tmra with his alternating boldness and timidity.

They were all different; they were all beautiful; and Ythiris loved them all to pieces.

AGAMENJIYR NJI MADUBABAKAR, King of Ordyuk, cared deeply both about his children and about his kingdom.

If asked, he would have considered those two cares one and the same: if his children flourished, his kingdom would as well; if his kingdom flourished, so would his children.

He had great faith in his children. His eldest, although the boy was recalcitrant and had a considerable temper, had already proven himself as being more than worthy of inheriting the throne; his daughter would become an excellent queen that any king would be blessed and fortunate to have by his side; his second son would become a legendary warrior; his youngest, while still a small child, was keenly perceptive and uncannily intuitive and would make a valuable adviser.

King Agamenjiyr had great faith in the future of Ordyuk.

DIYOMENDON HATED EVERYONE. His parents, his siblings, the citizens of Ordyuk, the people outside of Ordyuk—everyone in the entire world.

He hated his father for trying to make him become him. He hated his mother for always misunderstanding his anger and trying to reassure him that he'd make a great king. He hated his sister Naliki for following him around and not being bothered by his hatred. He hated his brother Luxanthus for always accepting things as they were and not hating him in return. He hated his brother Rezekyrios for being afraid of him.

He hated his academic instructors for being hard on him. He hated his fighting instructors for going easy on him. He hated the people of Ordyuk for being so stupid and sheeplike that they needed a king to lead them. He hated that it had to be him. He hated the people outside of Ordyuk for making the existence of the kingdom necessary. He hated the deities for making the world the way it was and for forcing him to be the way he was.

He hadn't asked to be born the Crown Prince of Ordyuk. He didn't care about being the Crown Prince of Ordyuk. He didn't want to be the Crown Prince of Ordyuk. It was, all of it, absolutely unfair, and it made him so *angry*.

NALIKI LOVED ALL HER BROTHERS, but she was closest with her elder brother. He was endlessly entertaining, and he made her feel special because she was the only one aside from their mother he allowed to call him Tdroki, while everyone else had to call him Diyomendon. Even if he told her not to and didn't call her Rkalla in return, he still let her get away with it.

He told her that he hated her, and she laughed at him because he didn't mean it and she knew it. So it didn't bother her any. She honestly preferred Tdroki's fiery and unforgiving temper to Nkidu's unflappable placidity or Tmra's fluctuating skittishness. Nkidu was unfailingly considerate, but he was boring as sand. It was easy to get rises out of young Tmra, but he was so sensitive that Naliki always felt bad for messing with him.

She could mess with Tdroki all she wanted, though, and he'd always get amusingly angry at her, and she didn't have to feel bad about it at all because that was just how he was.

LUXANTHUS WASN'T PARTICULARLY close with either of his older siblings. He didn't dislike either of them, but he also didn't and couldn't connect with them.

They completely baffled him, honestly. It seemed that no matter what he did, Diyomendon was always angry with him for something. Luxanthus could never figure out what he'd done wrong. And as far as his sister Naliki was concerned, Luxanthus had no idea how to interact with her. He couldn't tell what she expected from him. She seemed always disappointed with him for some reason.

Outside of royal and social obligations, Luxanthus therefore mostly kept to himself. That only changed once Tmra learned to walk and started following him around everywhere. Luxanthus was almost never alone, after that; Tmra tripped over himself to keep up with him no matter where he went.

The younger boy looked up to him; and when Tmra smiled at

him like he was the sun, it made Luxanthus feel like he could do anything.

REZEKYRIOS WAS MORE than a little frightened of his oldest brother, and his sister intimidated him. Being around them made him anxious. It was the way Diyomendon looked at him like he wanted to set him on fire and watch him burn alive, and the way Naliki smiled at him like she wanted to suck his blood.

Diyomendon would never have allowed Rezekyrios to call him Tdroki. Naliki insisted that Rezekyrios call her Rkalla, but it always felt weird to do so.

Rezekyrios adored his older brother Nkidu, though. Nkidu was kind, and he was strong, and he was good at everything. Rezekyrios felt completely safe whenever he was with him.

Nkidu was the best, and Rezekyrios wanted to be just like him.

YTHIRIS COULD GAUGE her children's relationships by which names they used with each other. In the Ordyukian culture, individuals' middle names were terms of intimacy and endearment used only by one's immediate family or the closest and most trusted of friends, while with the rest of society one's formal first name was used.

Her eldest son held a deliberate distance from his siblings by only using their first names and insisting they use his. Her daughter used all her siblings' middle names, even her older brother's, despite his demands that she not. Ythiris's second and third sons used their middle names with each other and their sister but acquiesced to the eldest's desire for a formal distance, although her youngest son also used his sister's formal name when referring to her outside of her company.

Ythiris herself used their middle names when she spoke with them, while her husband used their first names. Agamenjiyr was the king, and his responsibility to the kingdom had to come first. As the queen, Ythiris had more flexibility and could let herself indulge in motherhood with her children. She could be queen and mother equally, but Agamenjiyr had to be more king than father.

She suspected that it was the reason of his eventual succession to the throne that Tdroki used his siblings' formal names, already anticipating the distance that was necessary for the duties of a king. It made sense to Ythiris, though, that Rkalla would insist on using even Tdroki's middle name. The girl was unapologetically brazen and liked getting close to people and up under their skin. Nkidu, for his part, was flexible and could roll with anything, whether formal or intimate; but it made sense that Tmra would feel uncomfortable with his sister, given how sensitive he was.

Yet even despite their differences, they seemed to get along, with no lasting quarrels, and Ythiris felt herself blessed to have such wonderful, beautiful, gifted children.

ALL KING AGAMENJIYR'S children had their flaws.

Of course, they all had their merits, too, and their merits and flaws went closely hand-in-hand—but it was the flaws that he had to keep an eye on.

Diyomendon's temper and overall harsh demeanor, for instance. As king, the boy's strong opinions, vicious self-confidence, and aversion to being influenced by others would be a definite boon, but if he let his anger and unwillingness to listen to advice get the best of him, he could end up making poor decisions out of spite. His violent demeanor could also cost him the trust and loyalty of his subjects, who needed to feel that their king had the best interests of the kingdom and citizens at heart and would do everything in his power to secure their safety and livelihoods.

Naliki was confrontational and liked to push boundaries. These were not necessarily unfavorable qualities for a woman, especially if she were married strategically to an important member of the government or military whom she could help manipulate for the kingdom's benefit—she and Diyomendon were close, and Agamenjiyr felt assured that this would continue even once she was married and Diyomendon became king—but if she were too careless and pushed too far, she could get herself in trouble and take the kingdom down with her.

Luxanthus was the least glaringly flawed of Agamenjiyr's children, probably because his athletic and combative talent shone so brightly it blotted most else out, and because he was so quiet and reserved that it was impossible to tell what he was thinking or feeling; but there was a passivity to his nature that concerned Agamenjiyr. Certainly, having such a powerful warrior who so readily followed orders would be a blessing to any king, and the boy's self-possessed disposition would be of immeasurable worth in any crisis. Still, Agamenjiyr worried that, in his determination to carry out his duty no matter the cost, Luxanthus might too quickly accept and devote himself to an unfavorable or even fatalistic course of action rather than trying to find a better one.

It was Rezekyrios who concerned Agamenjiyr most. The boy was sensitive and nervous and, despite the clear keenness of his mind, there wasn't anything that he was particularly good at. He was astonishingly uncoordinated and clumsy, almost constantly tripping, crashing into things, knocking things over, and driving his fight instructors to their wits' ends with his incompetence. According to his academic tutors, he was quick on the uptake but had great difficulty focusing; and while he seemed to have an uncanny ability to memorize things and recite them by rote, when asked to evaluate material or explain something in his own words, he could barely string together a coherent sentence. It was uncertain what benefit he would be able to bring to Ordyuk.

Fortunately, Rezekyrios was Agamenjiyr's third son, and not necessary for the governing of the kingdom. As king, Agamenjiyr had a great number of much more pressing concerns.

But it was a concern to him nonetheless, both as a father and as a king. All of Agamenjiyr's children would have to learn to negotiate the world as their royal status dictated, and none of them—not even his youngest—was any exception.

DIYOMENDON, DESPITE HIS INCREDIBLE TEMPER, had excellent self-control. People really didn't give him enough credit for it. If they'd known how much rage he kept tightly bottled inside, they would've been both terrified and awed.

People thought he was angry and lashing out all the time. They hadn't even seen him lashing out. What they'd seen was him keeping his rage carefully, determinedly restrained. What they saw as him being intentionally vitriolic was him trying his hardest not to be. *That* was how vast his fury was.

They should all bless the Daimmu for his incredible self-control. The only times he allowed his anger out were when he was alone in his room.

Or at least, mostly alone. Sometimes his sister Naliki was there. He always shouted at her to leave, but she never did. He would upturn furniture and throw objects at the walls—but never at her.

She hadn't asked for any of this, either.

"If you don't want to be the Crown Prince, Tdroki—"

"It's *Diyomendon.*"

"—then what do you want to be? What would be better than this?"

She was sitting on his bed, smiling at him and swinging her bare feet.

Diyomendon glared at her. There was such a fire in his chest. It felt like it was burning him alive from the inside.

"What I want," he gritted out, "is for you to leave me alone."

"It seems to me," she told him, "that nothing would make you happy."

The flames within him roared. "And why," he said quietly, with a barely controlled rage that made his entire body shake, "should I want to be happy?"

He crowded into her space, placed a hand on either side of her legs on the bed, and leaned in, snarling. "Why is it so wrong for me to feel so angry?"

He hated that not only were there all these burdensome expectations about what he was supposed to *do*, but also all these burdensome expectations about how he was supposed to *feel*, and he found it terribly ironic that he was being raised to become the king and control the kingdom, when those same people who were raising him to become the king were trying to control him both from without and from within.

NALIKI KNEW THAT a lot of people found her older brother scary, but she'd never been frightened of him. She'd always known that he didn't actually hate her and that he would never hurt her.

When Tdroki leaned in close and demanded in desperate, abject fury why it was so wrong for him to feel angry, Naliki looked back at him with wide eyes for a moment and then grinned.

"Well, if you want to be angry, that's okay then," she'd reassured him, patting him on the cheek before ducking under his arm and skipping across the room. "Because that must mean that even if you hate it here, you must like it, since you like that you hate it. And if that's the case, then there's no one else you'd rather be!"

Which meant that there wasn't anyone he'd rather be than her brother, which made her happy because she liked having him as her brother.

It also meant that he'd always be angry about everything no matter what, and Naliki found that incredibly reassuring. No matter what might happen in their lives, she'd always be able to count on

Tdroki's anger. She thought that, as long as she could count on that, she wouldn't have to worry about anything.

He'd been fifteen at the time, she fourteen. They'd already been close, but they only continued to grow closer after that.

BY THE TIME he was thirteen, Luxanthus was able to beat most of the warriors in the Ordyukian Army one-on-one.

His instructors were having difficulty keeping him challenged. So he would be put under grueling physical training and then made to fight while exhausted. He would fight against an ever-increasing number of opponents, with warriors being added to the throng until he finally succumbed. They of course did not kill or grievously wound him, but they did make sure that he did not get out unscathed, in order that he would understand the consequences of defeat.

It was not easy, but neither was it more difficult than he could stand. He simply picked himself up from the sand, made a mental note of his mistakes, and tried again, with the intention of being better the next time. He understood that it was only natural that he would make mistakes and be overwhelmed out of inexperience, but he wanted to make sure that he never made the same mistake twice, and that he would develop himself to the point where what used to overwhelm him no longer fazed him. He couldn't do anything about what life threw at him, but he could do a lot about how he handled it; and as long as he could do something, he would.

It greatly cheered him when his six-year-old brother Tmra was waiting at the edge of the training arena with a glass of water, a cloth to wipe away his sweat, and a delighted grin beneath his shining mismatched eyes.

"That was so cool, Nkidu!"

The young boy was so genuine in his admiration that Luxanthus smiled, taking the water and cloth gratefully and ruffling the boy's messy hair.

"Thanks, Tmra."

That look on his younger brother's face made his exhaustion more than worth it, and made Luxanthus determined to continue becoming better.

REZEKYRIOS MAY HAVE BEEN only six, and Nkidu may have obviously been a natural talent when it came to fighting and physical feats, but even Rezekyrios knew that Nkidu's intense training must have started when he'd been around Rezekyrios's age.

And yet, Rezekyrios's own training was minimal and light.

Rezekyrios couldn't tell if this was because, with how talented Nkidu was, they simply didn't need him as a warrior, or if it was because he was such a natural klutz—being barely able to wield a wooden practice sword without hitting himself in the face—that they'd already given up on him.

He knew that he was awkward. His body felt lopsided, and he couldn't wrap his mind around how to force his strangely foreign limbs to perform the actions his instructors demonstrated to him. Surely that was the case for everyone in the beginning, and could be trained away? But his instructors looked at him as if they couldn't understand how he could be having such difficulties.

Rezekyrios couldn't understand it, either.

His academic education was likewise far lighter than Diyomendon's, and Rezekyrios didn't know if that was because, as the third son, he didn't need to be educated about the affairs of state, or if it was because he was so bad at learning, being barely able to focus on anything. He was easily distracted and easily agitated. It was difficult to concentrate on the words on the pages in front of him, or the words being spoken to him, when there were so many other sounds assaulting his ears, feeling like physical strikes and scratches; when the chair was uncomfortable and he couldn't figure out how to position his body to make it better; when the light in the room was so painful to his eyes that he fought not to clench them shut; when the dark ink on the pale parchment shifted like shivering sand, quaking as if the words would bury themselves in the grains of the page like scorpions; when there were small bright spots flashing everywhere in his peripheral vision, attracting his attention, and he couldn't stop trying to glance at them; when his instructors' every disappointed look and tone was a crushing blow leaving his mind in pieces that he had to scramble to collect back together again.

Nkidu always picked himself back up, even when he was ground into the dirt. He picked himself up, and there was such an unwavering look of determination in his eyes as he reached again for his weapon in the sand beside him.

Nkidu made everything look easy.

"Do you think I can be as strong as you, Nkidu?"

Nkidu looked at him like he was surprised by the question. "Of course."

"How do you know?" Rezekyrios had been worrying at his lower lip, feeling wretched, but Nkidu's eyes had softened and his lips had curved.

"You're my little brother, aren't you?" Nkidu then picked him up and spun him around, tossed him up into the air and then caught him again.

His older brother's smile was as bright as the sun. "You can do anything, Tmra."

Rezekyrios had thrown his arms around his brother's neck and buried his face in his shoulder.

He loved the warmth of the sun, but its light had always hurt his eyes.

ORDYUK WAS A HOT, desert kingdom located on the River Aru, the banks of which were deposited with fertile black sediment each flood season, making for excellent farming despite the surrounding arid landscape.

Due to the heat, the clothing worn there was light, simple, and minimal. Most people wore linen, but for those who worked with fire, such as the glassblowers who created the elaborate glass sculptures for which Ordyuk was known, it was necessary to wear a material that wouldn't easily go up in flame.

Women and children wore the same simple loincloths and kilts as the men, although women might also wear full-length, wrap-around linen gowns. Most people went barefoot, though at times sandals made of papyrus or leather would be worn, most especially by the warriors. The upper class and nobility wore much the same as the lower classes, except that their kilts were pleated and stitched with embroidery, their dresses were jeweled and beaded, and they adorned themselves with elaborate gold and beaded jewelry (as opposed to the copper pieces of the lower classes, which were strung with simpler materials like beads made from shells, clay, or colored glass). The amount and quality of jewelry worn was one's primary indication of status.

Appearance was important in Ordyuk. The epitome of masculine beauty was to have broad shoulders, a slim body, and muscular arms and legs; while the epitome of feminine beauty was to have a small waist, a flat stomach, and rounded breasts. Both men and women were expected to pay careful attention to hygiene and cleanliness, washing daily, wearing clean clothes, and making use of perfumes, deodorants, and toothpastes. Cosmetics were used by both men and women to enhance both personal appearance and health, helping to soften the skin, preserve a youthful appearance, and prevent wrinkling, as well as protect the body from the sun, ward off insects, shield the eyes from infection, and improve self-esteem.

Before her children were old enough to do so on their own, Ythiris applied first sun-shielding cream to their skin and then makeup, drawing with kohl in thick, dark lines around their eyes, emphasizing their size and shape. They were her Gem Children, and she chose their jewelry accordingly: carnelian-adorned pieces for her fiery Tdroki and his carnelian eyes; pieces inset and beaded with garnet and obsidian for her bold, garnet-eyed Rkalla; pieces set with deep-blue lapis lazuli to bring out the sunlike shine of her tranquil Nkidu's gold eyes; pieces inlaid with black obsidian and honey-yellow amber to complement both the light and the dark eye of her thoughtful Tmra.

When they kept wearing the kinds of jewelry that she'd picked out for them even after they were old enough to choose their own, Ythiris didn't say anything, but it did make her smile as she watched them grow and shine, evolving the styles into their own as they matured.

MOST JOBS IN ORDYUK were inherited: whatever job your father had, you had.

However, if one was low on the social ladder and wanted to move up, one could become a scribe or join the army. Anyone could join the army. Of course, it was carefully ranked, and the highest positions were inherited and passed down from father to son. But anyone could become a foot soldier. With enough effort, they could raise themselves in the ranks. The army was large and highly organized, with an efficient bureaucracy that made sure it was fully supplied and operations ran smoothly.

One of the king's jobs was to direct this army in times of foreign threat or internal conflict. Generally speaking, the king's primary job was to take care of his people. The king owned the land, made the laws, and collected taxes in the form of grain that was kept in storehouses for the event of a famine. The king was also the kingdom's high priest, representing the Daimmu, the deities of the elements to which the people of Ordyuk owed their fortune and livelihoods. The king, as the high priest, dedicated temples in the Daimmu's honor and performed sacred rituals.

Agamenjiyr had been fulfilling these duties as king for nearly as long as he could remember, having inherited the throne as a child after his father's untimely death. He hoped not to inflict the same fate so early on his son. Following his death, it would be Diyomendon's turn to be the King of Ordyuk.

Agamenjiyr wanted to make sure that Diyomendon was well prepared for that day, when it came.

DIYOMENDON WAS THE CROWN PRINCE, and his life, health, and body were sacred.

Whenever he made a mistake, it was not he who paid the price, but his younger brother Luxanthus. Every mistake that Diyomendon made on an evaluation was another lap around the city that Luxanthus had to run, another opponent added to the number that Luxanthus had to fight, and another hour that Luxanthus had to train into the night when everyone else was sleeping.

Diyomendon hated it. It wasn't fair.

"It's not fair," Agamenjiyr agreed, looking at him with steady eyes. "That's what it means to be king: every mistake that you make is paid for by your subjects."

Diyomendon's fists were clenched so hard they trembled.

"Why don't you make Luxanthus king?!" he demanded one day. "He does everything right!"

Agamenjiyr shook his head. "Luxanthus is excellent at following orders. But a king needs to be able to think for himself."

Diyomendon's rage surged. "You're cutting Luxanthus short, Father. He's not some simple-minded idiot who's simply following orders. He evaluates everything carefully and then takes the best course of action given the circumstances."

"Luxanthus takes the safest course of action," Agamenjiyr said.

"He doesn't take risks. A king needs to be willing to risk loss in order to gain. For his kingdom's sake."

He looked at Diyomendon keenly. "The entirety of Ordyuk is going to be yours, Diyomendon. The fate of the kingdom and its people are going to be resting on you."

Diyomendon trembled, barely able to restrain his rage. He didn't want to rule the kingdom.

He wanted to burn it to the ground.

NALIKI WOULD EVENTUALLY become the wife of a distinguished member of the Ordyukian nobility, either in the government or in the upper ranks of the military. Her mother, smiling, gave her tips.

"Men are physically strong, but they're mentally weak," her mother told her. "They're easily influenced, especially by a woman; if you play your cards right, you'll have your husband dancing to your beat. No matter how much power he has, you will be the one behind it."

Naliki grinned in response.

She always had felt powerful.

She practiced on her brothers, sometimes. They weren't physically attracted to her, being her siblings, which was an obvious disadvantage, but she could still manipulate their simple minds to a degree.

Tdroki didn't really care what he was angry about, as long as he was angry, so it was easy for her to redirect his anger from one thing to something else. Nkidu had a great desire to do everything right, and it was almost frighteningly easy to influence him by telling him what was right and expected and what was wrong and disparaged.

It was only her youngest brother who gave her trouble, really. In his responses, she found him wholly unpredictable. Sometimes he was completely oblivious, but sometimes he was so sensitive. He was easily hurt, and he looked so sad when he was that she couldn't help but hug him and tell him she was sorry. He flinched when she did, and she found that it pained her in a way she couldn't explain.

Perhaps, though, that was what it meant to be an older sibling: that feeling of responsibility for a younger sibling's feelings. She'd never felt that way with Nkidu, given that he was so self-sufficient it was almost disturbing. But with Tmra it was different. Naliki felt accountable for him and protective. If anyone degraded Tdroki or Nkidu, she laughed at them for being ignorant—but if they degraded Tmra, she found herself ready to rip out throats.

Maybe it was the fact that he was significantly younger than the rest of them, or maybe it was the fact that sometimes he looked at her like he was looking through her completely; but while she could laugh at both Tdroki and Nkidu for their pain, she only wanted to kiss Tmra's away.

Still, he shied from her like she would stab him, and she didn't understand why.

"Why is Tmra so scared of me?" she'd asked Nkidu once, since Nkidu was closest to Tmra.

Nkidu had looked at her with his unreadable sunlight eyes. "He probably doesn't understand what you want from him." He'd shrugged, and Naliki had pursed her lips.

"What doesn't he understand?"

Nkidu had shrugged again and looked at her like the midday sun would regard the deepest hours of midnight.

LUXANTHUS LIKED TO GO up on the palace roof at night. It was large and flat, and a great place to train in solitude, or to simply take a moment to relax and look up at the colorful night sky or out over the city.

He was sitting on the edge of the roof one night when he heard footsteps behind him. He almost didn't recognize them as his older brother's, they were so quiet. Diyomendon usually stomped.

His older brother sat down next to him. Luxanthus had his feet hanging over the edge and was leaning back slightly on his hands, but Diyomendon sat with his legs crossed, slumping and hunching his shoulders, seemingly simply because he could. No one was watching who would tell him not to.

Luxanthus glanced at him. Luxanthus wore less jewelry than his siblings since he was usually training, which meant he also generally wore the trousers that were characteristic of the Bardyuk martial art he practiced: made of light linen, loose but drawn tight at the waist and ankles. Diyomendon, for whom physical training was only a small part of his expansive educational regime, was wearing the more royalty-typical decorated kilt that went down to his knees and was tied around his waist with a sash, and he was fully adorned in extensive gold jewelry: rings and bangles, necklaces, an elaborate beaded collar-piece, and dangling earrings.

The carnelian stones glinted in the night. Diyomendon's glare was fiercer. "I came here for the quiet. If you say anything, you can go die."

Luxanthus shifted his gaze away and didn't say anything. He looked out over the sleeping city with its mudbrick, flat-topped buildings. He wanted to run along the roofs and jump between them, like a leopard.

It wouldn't have been allowed.

"Why don't you resent me for it?" The night had been dark and serene; Diyomendon's tone was darker, angry and bitter.

Luxanthus glanced back over at him, wondering if talking was allowed now that Diyomendon had spoken. "For what?"

The older boy was looking down and jabbing at the roof in front of him with a finger, as if he were crushing ants. There were no ants. "You have to pay the price for all my mistakes."

Luxanthus blinked at him. "I don't think of it like that," he said truthfully.

"Oh?" Diyomendon was fierce and challenging as he met

Luxanthus's gaze aslant. "And how do you think of it, then?"

Luxanthus looked back at him easily. "It makes me stronger." The fact that the punishments for his older brother's mistakes were bitter increases to the intensity of his own training was a lesson to both of them: that Diyomendon was directly responsible for the lives of those under his rule, and that it was Luxanthus's duty to make up for the inevitable instances of his human error. Every time the heir made a mistake, Luxanthus was forced to work harder: the harder he worked, the stronger he became. This was how he'd become strong enough to support his older brother once Diyomendon became king.

"Tch." Diyomendon looked away, crushing nonexistent ants on the roof. His spiky hair looked like black flame against the luminous night sky behind him. Luxanthus glanced back at the city and felt glad that mudbrick didn't burn.

It was quiet between them again. Luxanthus wondered why Diyomendon was sitting with him like this. Maybe he simply had also been having trouble sleeping. The roof was nice, and it was better to be sleepless in company.

He heard the angry hiss of breath that indicated his older brother was about to speak, before Diyomendon said, "Father basically called you an idiot, the other day."

Luxanthus blinked, looking over at him again. "And?"

Diyomendon glared at him, furious for some reason, and then looked away with the same ferocity as a jackal tearing flesh from bone. "Tch." He jabbed at the roof. "I mean, I understand why people think you're duller than sand, when you act like that. But you're no idiot."

Luxanthus watched him for a few moments, and then looked back out over the city. He wasn't concerned with what people thought about him, but it seemed to be important to Diyomendon.

Luxanthus shifted his gaze past the city to the dark expanse of desert beyond the defensive walls. "Sand can be bright, you know," he reminded his brother. "When it's in the sun. And when you look closely at a handful of it, you can see that it has many colors in it. Even though it looks solid tan from a distance."

In his periphery, he saw Diyomendon stop jabbing at the roof, and he could feel the weight of his brother's gaze on the side of his face. Luxanthus looked over questioningly.

Diyomendon was staring at him, uncharacteristically dumbfounded. "…You should've been born the son of a poet."

Luxanthus blinked at him. "I enjoy the training," he pointed out. "And the fighting."

"Do you?" Diyomendon was looking at him askance.

Luxanthus shrugged, shifting his gaze away again. It felt good to use his body and push it to its limits. It felt good, too, knowing that as a warrior he'd have the power to help defend the kingdom. He'd never feel locked-up and powerless to do anything, the way he knew his older brother felt.

"It means I don't have to bottle up my frustration," he said. "I can let it out." The words 'Unlike you' went unsaid, but Diyomendon heard them anyway.

He snarled at Luxanthus. "I hate you."

Luxanthus looked up at the sky and its countless stars. "I know." He didn't particularly care what other people thought about him.

Diyomendon sneered, and stood up to leave. "If you keep coming up here, you're going to get caught eventually, you know."

Luxanthus's lips curved. "I can handle the punishment that would be dealt out for it." The more difficult they made it on him, the stronger he'd get. And he wanted to become as strong as he could. He tilted his head back to look at his older brother's retreating figure. "So you can come up here as much as you like too, you know. Even at the risk of your getting caught." He meant it.

Diyomendon went rigid, turning slightly to glare at him over his shoulder. "Go die." Then Diyomendon's bearing loosened and he threw his head back in a laugh. "Ha! Maybe then you'd actually get some rest."

Luxanthus felt tired, but not physically. It was only in his head. "You're no idiot either, Diyomendon." He wished his older brother would stop mentally beating himself up about things that he didn't need to beat himself up over.

Diyomendon gritted his teeth and glared at him. "Jump off the roof you're dangling your dirty feet over, Luxanthus."

"They're not dirty," Luxanthus said automatically; he'd washed them right before turning in for bed, and then coming up to the roof.

Still, thinking about the rest of his older brother's statement, Luxanthus found himself sitting up to look over the edge of the roof, wondering idly if he'd survive the fall if he did jump.

"If you're actually considering doing that, then you really are an idiot, Luxanthus!"

Luxanthus smiled slightly. "I bet you I'd survive it."

"Not without at least one broken bone, you sand-head!"

Luxanthus shrugged, smile broadening. "Bones heal," he pointed out.

Diyomendon hissed behind him. "Then jump, for all I care." Luxanthus looked back at him to see Diyomendon turn and start walking away again, waving a hand that jingled with gold bracelets and glittered with gold rings. "—And then when they pick you up in the morning, go ahead and tell them I ordered you to do it!"

Luxanthus frowned slightly. "I wouldn't do that," he said.

"Well, maybe you should," Diyomendon snapped back, without pausing in his angry stride.

Luxanthus was left looking after him and wondering what he had meant by that.

IN THE DESERT, the rains that brought the flooding of the Aru River, which made the growing of crops along its bank possible, were sacred. Every year, the first rains were celebrated with a festival to Nimuru, the Daimu of the Sky, Wind, Air, Storms, and Rain.

There was a traditional rain dance that was performed to honor Nimuru. The dance was full of fluid, liquid movements with fantastic, energetic, and explosive outbursts. The coordination it required was great.

Naliki and Nkidu were participating. Diyomendon had refused.

Rezekyrios hadn't been allowed. He couldn't perform those moves. He would have looked like a dying praying mantis and slipped in the rain and fallen on his face, embarrassing the royal family.

King Agamenjiyr and Queen Ythiris, being the high priest and priestess, were also participating in the dance. Which meant that it was just Rezekyrios and his eldest brother Diyomendon standing on the side, watching.

The king and queen were practiced, and their movements were flawless, but it was clear that the dancing of Naliki and Nkidu was something special. They were decked in gold and deep-blue lapis lazuli to honor the sky and the water, and the smoothness and energy of their movements made them look like the great Nimuru made flesh.

Rezekyrios's eyes ached, but he couldn't take his gaze away from them.

"How do they do it?" he wondered, quietly, chewing on his lower lip.

"How do they do what?" Diyomendon snapped from beside him. Diyomendon was leaning against the wall of a building, arms crossed over his bejeweled chest, and scowling. He looked like he might burst aflame with the intensity of his ire. His hair—like Nkidu's—seemed to defy the water that saturated it and still stuck up.

Rezekyrios swallowed thickly. Diyomendon always made him nervous. Even lower than before, he murmured, "How do they move like that?" He didn't understand how anyone could have such complete control over their body.

Diyomendon scoffed. "By being idiots," he said, harsh and contemptuous.

It made Rezekyrios blink in abject surprise and blurt out, louder than intended, "What?"

Diyomendon's mouth pulled in a sneer, and he waved his hand at the dancers on the raised dais derisively. "To be in your body like that, you have to let go of your mind: stop thinking."

Rezekyrios chewed on his lip, looking back at the dancers who moved and leapt like water.

"That's why you'll never be able to," Diyomendon added, flat and caustic. "You think far too much, Rezekyrios."

There was a crushing weight around Rezekyrios's chest. "That's a bad thing?" he murmured. He rubbed at his aching eyes. There were puddles around his bare feet, splashing and rippling in the rain. Rezekyrios was reminded of leopard fur.

Diyomendon snorted next to him. "Who am I to say? Some might say I also think too much. Pity for them." He looked down at Rezekyrios, his grin savage and his gaze burning. "Just be you, Rezekyrios. No point trying to be something you're not. You'll just fail."

Diyomendon's expression was like a showering of red-hot sparks on Rezekyrios's skin, and he flinched, turning his head away. He closed his eyes and tried to breathe and calm the pounding of his heart. Thoughts were flurrying in his head, and he hardly knew what he was saying as he started softly: "Do you..."

Diyomendon hissed impatiently. "Spit it out."

Rezekyrios was sure that he nearly choked on his own tongue. Wouldn't that have been a feat to add to his already astonishing list of incompetent failings. But he managed to more or less get out the burgeoning thought. "Do you feel like you're failing? In...in trying to become king?"

Rezekyrios bit hard on his lip; he was going to die, now. He rubbed at his eyes.

Diyomendon just snorted, though, not seeming to be any angrier than he always was. "Tch. I'm not trying to become king. I'm being made to be a king." Where Rezekyrios's gaze was on the ground, he saw his older brother kick harshly at a puddle, making it spray. "But I'll never be the kind of king that they all want." Diyomendon's tone was bitter and acrid as ash. "I'll never be like Father."

"So then..." Rezekyrios looked up at him, wondering. "Could you become the king that you want?"

Diyomendon's lips pulled back from his teeth like a hissing snake baring its fangs. *"I don't want to become king at all."* He turned his flaming gaze on Rezekyrios, and the younger boy flinched. The Crown Prince's tone was so dark. "You have more freedom than I do, Rezekyrios. You can basically do whatever you want."

Rezekyrios had looked back at his sister and brother dancing like the water itself was imbuing their bodies, and Diyomendon hissed and shoved him in the head, making him stumble.

"Stop looking at them and take a better look at yourself," the older boy snapped.

Keeping his head down, Rezekyrios lifted his aching eyes to look at the dancers from beneath the darkness of his eyebrows.

He could barely speak around his swollen tongue, the taste of blood in his mouth from accidentally biting it when he'd been shoved. "But the way they move is so cool..."

"So what?" Diyomendon said, callous. His every exhale was like the crackling and spitting of fire. "Your eyeliner is smudged, by the way." He knocked Rezekyrios's hand away from his face. "You need to stop rubbing at your eyes."

Rezekyrios lowered his hand. "They hurt," he said quietly.

Diyomendon scoffed. "Then let them hurt. But don't you dare

cry."

"I'm not," Rezekyrios said, feeling a bite of indignation. His eyes hurt, but it wasn't the sting of tears. He knew better than to cry.

"Good," Diyomendon said. There was silence between them, filled thickly with the sound of rain and the music accompanying the dancers, before Diyomendon broke through it with another hissing breath. "By Nimuru, is it wet," he grumbled, and when Rezekyrios looked up at him he was raising his head and trying to see over the crowd. "Where's some fire?"

"Inside you?" Rezekyrios said it without thinking, and his heartbeat rose as Diyomendon froze and then looked down at him, flaming eyes narrowing.

"Not you, too," he muttered, low and dark, and Rezekyrios was confused.

"What?" He couldn't help but ask, even though he felt like it would get him burned.

Diyomendon just shook his head, though, like a wet and angry cat furious at being unable to rid itself of the water. "Poets, the lot of you," he said bitterly, waving a hand. "Forget it." He shifted his gaze away, and then his eyes lit up. "Aha, there's some fire." He took off into the dense crowd with the single-mindedness of a cheetah going after a gazelle. He called back, "Don't get lost or washed away, Tmra!"

Rezekyrios figured that Diyomendon had used his middle name so as not to attract attention to themselves and their identities, but it still paralyzed him. He struggled to find his limbs again and took off after his older brother, trying not to trip or slip or get left too far behind.

There were so many people. Rezekyrios was bumping into them, and they were bumping into him, and it was making his heartbeat pound in his ears even louder than the rain and the drums.

Luckily, his older brother hadn't gone far, and Rezekyrios was able to find him again after only a couple of panicked seconds.

When Rezekyrios made it out of the crowd and over to him, Diyomendon practically shoved a piece of cooked meat skewered on a stick into his face.

"Eat that and don't burn yourself doing it," Diyomendon ordered, and then moved surreptitiously closer to the fire that was being used to cook the meat at the awning-covered street stand he'd found. He glanced at the fire, then back out at the crowd dancing and laughing in the rain. He grabbed Rezekyrios's arm and pulled him closer, saying more quietly: "Eat it slowly so we have an excuse to stand here next to the fire."

Diyomendon didn't have one of the skewers of meat for himself, and when Rezekyrios looked at him curiously, his fiery gaze simply moved back to the flickering orange flames. "Needed to buy something for that excuse, but I'm not hungry," he muttered. He tugged Rezekyrios closer to him, under the awning out of the rain, and Rezekyrios went obediently but with his heart pounding.

Diyomendon wasn't really looking at him, though, keeping his gaze on the fire, so Rezekyrios took a bite from the hot meat. His mouth salivated in response. He hadn't realized he'd been hungry.

But his brother had said to eat slowly. Rezekyrios pointedly turned his gaze back out to the crowd in the rain to distract himself as he chewed. As he did, he noticed that his brother Nkidu had disappeared from the raised dais where the dancing was taking place.

Rezekyrios blinked, eyes scanning over the crowd. Movement in the sky caught his attention, and he looked up. He nearly choked on the bite of meat in his mouth.

Chewing and swallowing hurriedly, Rezekyrios reached out to tug on one of Diyomendon's gold bracelets.

"Hey, Diyo—Tdroki," he quickly corrected himself, remembering the way his older brother had used his middle name and figuring that he was supposed to do the same. Diyomendon turned his fiery eyes on him angrily but Rezekyrios pointed up, where a familiar figure was walking across a rope stretched taut between the roofs of the buildings above them. "Isn't that Nkidu?"

Diyomendon looked up, eyes landing on the figure and widening slightly. "...What is that idiot doing?"

As they watched, Nkidu, with his arms stretched out to his sides like steady wings, crossed to the building on the opposite side, and then began crossing back, walking backward across the rope while being drenched in water.

On the raised dais, Naliki was dancing solo. She rivaled the rain in her splendor.

"By all the Daimmu," Diyomendon spat, looking away, gaze falling back on the fire. His teeth were gritted and his fists were clenched. "Cursed show-offs."

Rezekyrios watched his eldest brother next to him, looked back up at his other older brother above him, looked back down at the skewered meat in his hand. "Our parents are going to be angry, aren't they?" he asked quietly.

They had all run off. He was pretty sure that none of them was supposed to be doing what they were.

Diyomendon sneered. "Let them," he said, vindictive. "Lux—" he broke himself off, correcting, "—*Nkidu* will take all the punishment for us. And he doesn't mind." The older boy's tone was dark and searing as coals, and Rezekyrios looked over at him, chewing his lip.

He knew that Nkidu wouldn't mind. Nothing bothered Nkidu. Nkidu could do anything.

It made Diyomendon so angry.

Rezekyrios's eyes were aching, but he stopped his hand when he caught himself reaching up to rub at them. "You mind," he said to Diyomendon, looking down. He could feel the rage radiating off the older boy like waves of heat. "You mind that he'll take the punishment."

Diyomendon snapped at him, "No, I don't."

The hissing breath Diyomendon let out said otherwise. He stared deep into the fire with the flames reflecting in his red-orange eyes and turning them to furnaces that could melt sand to glass. "Shut up and eat the food, Tmra." His tone lowered, almost a grumble, and his fingers were digging into the muscle of his crossed arms. "Just don't eat it too fast. Chew each bite a total of fifty times or something. It'll keep your mouth busy so you don't say stupid things."

Rezekyrios swallowed his saliva, took another bite of the meat, and started counting.

It calmed him.

THE RAINSTORM MADE the day nearly as dark as night.

Even in the luminescent dim, Ythiris's children glowed.

Her dear Rkalla and Nkidu had always been dancers: Rkalla moved with complete possession of her body and delighted in opportunities to be extravagant, and Nkidu's natural athletic talent applied to dancing as much as it applied to fighting; neither of them had any problems with participating in the dance to honor Nimuru. If anything, Rkalla had been excited to do so, and Nkidu had seen it as a part of his training and applied himself to the task of learning the dance with his characteristic seriousness.

The way they danced, they stole everyone's eyes. They glowed.

Tdroki could dance, but he hated it, and he hit the beats too hard. He had always, since he was old enough to do so, absolutely refused to participate in dances.

Ythiris suspected that it was at least partly because his youngest brother couldn't.

When Tmra tried to dance, he tripped over himself and grew painfully frustrated. Because of the image the royal family necessarily upheld, he would never have been allowed to participate in any of the dances. He was forced to watch. Tdroki didn't like things that weren't fair.

Tdroki watched with Rezekyrios—and also over him.

Agamenjiyr had tried to convince Tdroki to dance before, but Ythiris's eldest son had put his foot down. "Deal with it," he'd said. "When the Daimmu created the world, they didn't make it fair." Then he'd crossed over and taken his youngest brother by the hand, leading him out of the room. "Come on, Rezekyrios. Let's get away from all this music and dancing. There are deities other than Kulele."

Tdroki had always been protective of his younger siblings. It made Ythiris's heart ache and soar.

Rkalla and Nkidu danced; but although Tdroki and Tmra only watched, they glowed. It was the way Tdroki stood protectively next to his youngest brother; the way Tmra chased after him even into the crowds that he so hated; the way Tdroki fed the younger boy before feeding himself.

There was never any doubt in Ythiris's mind that Tdroki would grow up to become an incredible king, just like his father.

AGAMENJIYR WAS NOT an only child. His younger sister, once Kaluli Tsaru Madubabakar and now Kalulit Saru Anhessekesmet, was married to Ythiris's younger brother, Hathalszar Anhessekesmet, who was now Agamenjiyr's most trusted adviser.

Agamenjiyr knew what it was like to have a younger sibling whom one felt responsible for. Since he had ascended to the throne at such a young age, he'd had precious little free time to enjoy with her.

He'd had precious little free time to enjoy himself at all.

Agamenjiyr was not resentful. He'd done what was necessary for the kingdom, had fulfilled his duty and fulfilled it well. He was proud to have done so. He was proud to still be doing so. It brought him great satisfaction and gratification to serve his duty as the King of Ordyuk.

He could not help, though, but wish to allow his children to have some of those moments that he had never had as a youth.

That was not to say that he went easy on them. With the responsibilities they would shoulder as royalty, they could not afford his being lax with them. Both their fates and the fate of the Kingdom of Ordyuk rested on how well they understood their roles and were trained in their duties.

But he found himself allowing them moments. They would be punished for them, later, so that they would understand that such actions would always come with consequences. But he did not immediately put a stop to them. It was better that they experience both those moments of shirking their duties and the ramifications of them, than to never experience either.

That was why, during the annual Rain Festival, when Diyomendon and Rezekyrios ran off, Agamenjiyr let them; that was why, when the music stopped but Naliki kept dancing, improvising solo and forcing the musicians to start up again to keep up with her, Agamenjiyr allowed it; that was why, when Luxanthus leapt up onto the roof of a nearby building and started walking across a rope stretched taut over the street, Agamenjiyr didn't call him down.

He would have done those things if he'd thought his children's actions would have consequences beyond those of the punishment he would mete out. But he trusted Diyomendon and Rezekyrios to keep each other out of trouble, Naliki's dancing was truly a sight to behold and would not anger Nimuru, and as for Luxanthus—with anyone else, Agamenjiyr and all those watching would've been afraid someone walking across a rope in the rain would fall.

With Luxanthus, they could only watch in wondering awe.

The boy was something truly phenomenal—blessed by the Daimmu themselves—and he gave everyone around him the capti-vating feeling of assurance that there was nothing he couldn't accomplish, no matter how inhuman the feat. One looked at him, and one felt like one was witnessing the beginnings of a legend.

So Agamenjiyr allowed his children this undisciplined behavior, because Diyomendon and Rezekyrios were both so high-strung they could use a moment to relax, because Naliki and Luxanthus had such boundless energy they could use a moment to let go, and because all the people of Ordyuk who saw Naliki dancing and Luxanthus crossing that wire in the rain would—like Agamenjiyr himself—be filled with faith that the Daimmu would continue to be kind and there could be no threat to the kingdom that would not be unequivocally crushed.

IT WAS SHORTLY AFTER the Rain Festival that the enigmatic old man made his appearance in the throne room, where the king received messengers and conducted business.

Diyomendon had been shadowing his father at the time, observing the king at his daily duties. He hated it less than he hated lessons, and he hated that he consequently always felt relieved at the chance, which ended up making his anger level about the same.

He was already stewing in fury, therefore, when the old man came in escorted by two guards, one of whom announced, "This man calls himself 'Aiy-yodd-healb-hachk-sinn-gann'." The guard said the name carefully, tripping over the foreign sounds. "He insisted on seeing you, Your Excellency."

The old man was tan and wrinkled, with frazzled white hair and beard and a jagged scar over his left eye. He wore a strange blue robe wrapped around his wiry body that was tied around his waist with a thin sash, and he walked with a slight hunch. He carried a gnarled wooden walking stick that nearly matched his gnarled and scarred hands.

Diyomendon hated him for his very existence and for intruding on their matters. He knew that if some random, ancient-looking foreigner had insisted on seeing the King of Ordyuk, the matter had to either be foolishly trivial or monumentally dire. Neither option was agreeable.

King Agamenjiyr regarded the old foreigner with narrowed gold-orange eyes in a much younger and smoother face, his hair still colored with deep, bronze-stroked browns. "You may speak."

The old man bowed respectfully. In a drafty but steady voice, he asked, "Has your kingdom been having trouble with any monsters, recently?"

The question was either presumptuous goading or an oblique portent, and it made Diyomendon's rage blaze.

The old man could go die, or say what he meant straight out.

"No," the king answered, his eyes narrowing further. "In what way does it concern you, Stratva-Master Aodhealbhach Sinngan of Niran?" Agamenjiyr's tongue flowed with much more practice over the foreign name than the guard's had, and he clearly knew who the old man was. Diyomendon moved his own narrowed stare between the two of them.

The old man bowed again. "I was just wondering. I'm deeply sorry for bothering you. Thank you considerably for your time."

Then he left.

Once he was gone, Diyomendon turned his incensed gaze on his father. "You know him. Or else you know of him."

The king leaned his cheek on his fist, regarding the doors to the chamber through which the old man had entered and then left. "He's a master of the Stratva martial art and leads the prodigious dojo in the village of Niran, between the northern edge of the Ririan Forest and the base of the Heidien Mountains," Agamenjiyr said. There was distrust and misgiving in his voice.

Diyomendon glanced at the doors as well, and then looked back to regard his father. "You're wondering what he's doing this far south," he stated, "and what he meant by asking if we've been having trouble with monsters."

"It makes me uneasy," the king agreed. He straightened in his throne, waving his hand. "No matter." Louder, he called to the guards at the doors across the hall, "Show in the next visitor."

The matter was deemed irrelevant and brushed aside, apart from a lingering flame in Diyomendon's chest: one more thing to hate about the world, among all the rest that had gathered there and together composed the blistering fire of his being.

It was shortly after that that the monsters started showing up, and that flame in Diyomendon's chest roared into a raging conflagration that felt as if it could consume him.

If only he could have taken all that flaming hatred and fury, turned it on the monsters, and burned them to ash, instead of having nowhere to turn it but inside, where he was the only one whom it burned alive.

II

THE MONSTERS WERE known generally as the Accursed, as their monstrous state was the product of a curse from the Chaos Deity, Jajul. Jajul was one of the three Ungarru who ruled Life's three underlying states: Chaos, Order, and Death. Along with Jajul, the other two Ungarru were Rujir and Injal, respectively. Unlike the Daimmu, the Ungarru were never on anyone's side.

The Accursed individuals—or else their ancestors—had once been human, and they looked like any other human, up until giant appendages resembling those of scorpions or spiders burst out of their bodies and their eyes became so bloodshot they gained the appearance of gouged-out sockets. Their teeth were sharp, and they hunted humans and consumed their flesh. If you happened to survive an Accursed's arachnoid appendage piercing your flesh, you would become one of them yourself.

The Accursed were the monsters that had brought about the Great Calamity a few decades before, the disaster in which Agamenjiyr's father had been killed, forcing Agamenjiyr onto the throne as a young child. They'd swarmed out of the southern desert in astonishing numbers, overwhelming the kingdom. Along with the previous king, almost half of the population of Ordyuk had been wiped out. The only reason it hadn't been even worse was because the other Daimmu had blessed the Ordyukian warriors with powers to help them fight against the monsters. Still, by the end, the country had been in shambles. King Agamenjiyr and his advisers had, with painstaking effort, finally rebuilt the kingdom to a state nearly equaling its former glory.

Now the Accursed were back. At the news, King Agamenjiyr and every other survivor of the Great Calamity paled. Many also dropped whatever they were holding, cursed, or started praying to the Daimmu.

The younger generations were alarmed, watching their parents and elders come undone. They'd heard about the Accursed and the Great Calamity, of course, but mostly in tales about the gifts of the Daimmu and the bravery of the Blessed Warriors who had saved the kingdom.

Of those Blessed Warriors who had survived the Great Calamity, none remained.

There had only been a handful of Accursed attacks thus far, and only at the edges of Ordyuk along the southern desert, but the fear of another devastating wave of them was growing, casting an anxious air over the kingdom. People were praying to the Daimmu, standing lookouts, checking people's teeth, boarding their doors at night, and avoiding travel in the dark when possible. Still, there was the faith that the Daimmu would protect them.

When the news of the Accursed's return had been brought to the palace, after the survivors had gone pale, every eye in the room had turned to Nkidu.

Nkidu, although only fourteen years of age, had straightened and said calmly, "What do you need me to do?"

Everyone had relaxed at his tone and attitude, Naliki included. If there was anyone who would be able to kill the creatures without a problem, it would be her not-so-little little brother. It had long been suspected that he'd been born a Blessed Warrior.

Still, he was young, and the Accursed were notoriously difficult to kill. Not only because of their giant arachnoid appendages that both were formidable weapons and allowed them to crawl up walls and move in other utterly inhuman ways, but also because the monsters purportedly had enhanced physical strength and speed and a significant regenerative ability. As a child, Naliki had seen likenesses of them in scrolls and wall-paintings, and even those artist-rendered images had been frightening enough to have the monsters crawling through her nightmares. Seeing them in person, when a few were captured alive for Nkidu to train against, had been even more terrifying.

She was fifteen years of age now. She wasn't a little girl any-more. She wasn't going to cry and cower with fear in the dark. She could push her fear down the same way Tdroki pushed down his anger—except better. She could pretend that she wasn't afraid at all, while Tdroki could try to smother the flames of his anger but still it curled from his very flesh like smoke.

And ever since the appearance of the Accursed, Tdroki had been furious. Fury emanated from him with such feverish intensity that sometimes Naliki expected him to smell of roasting flesh, as if it were burning him alive.

He didn't really smell of roasting flesh, though. When she wrapped her arms around him and buried her nose in his neck, he wasn't even feverish to the touch, and he smelled sweetly and spici-ly of perfume: myrrh, frankincense, pine resin, mastic, cinnamon, cardamom, saffron, juniper, and mint.

It was the same perfume they all used—although Nkidu, no matter how much deodorant he applied or how regularly he bathed, could never entirely rid himself of the lingering scent of sweat from his constant training.

That training had become even more intense, recently, as he'd begun learning to take down the Accursed. His academics had been abandoned completely in favor of fighting. The exercises, when Naliki dropped by, looked positively grueling. Their younger brother was being put under all this extra pressure now—and it wasn't even because of any mistake by Tdroki.

The older boy was so incredibly upset by it.

It was kind of funny to Naliki how Tdroki always insisted that he hated his sister and brother, when it was so obvious that he cared.

Tdroki had locked himself in his room, as he always did, but Naliki had long ago learned to pick locks for exactly this purpose.

She popped the lock of his door open, stepped inside, and closed and locked the door behind her.

Tdroki didn't bother trying to kick her out anymore.

The older boy was furiously pacing his room, teeth clenched and fingers gripped in his hair and tugging harshly. As if he could make it stand up any more than it already was.

He'd been furious silently, but once she entered, he started ranting out loud. It was endearing the way he always did that: narrating his thoughts for her.

"What was with that old man?! Asking if we were having any trouble with monsters, and then these monsters start showing up—! Is this all his fault?!"

Tdroki had already told Naliki about the foreigner. Tdroki told her everything.

"He was just some old, respected martial arts master from the northern mountains, right? Someone like that's not likely to have anything to do with Jajul and the Accursed, especially not when they come from the deep southern desert," she pointed out, hopping up to sit on his bed while she watched him pace. He was just angry and looking for someone to blame, but beneath his anger, he had to know as well as she did that what he was suggesting was highly unlikely. "The old martial arts guy probably just stumbled across some sign in his travels that the Accursed were starting to show up again and was trying to warn us, or was wondering if we were already having problems with them."

Tdroki seethed, fiery eyes outlined with charcoal-black kohl and blazing. "What kind of a needlessly obscure warning was that, then?! If he wanted to warn us, he could've actually told us! And then maybe also how we're supposed to deal with—!" In abject frustration, Tdroki whirled and slammed the side of a fist against the wall, letting out a hiss through gritted teeth. The gold and carnelian jewelry along his arm, shoulders, and chest jangled with the force of the strike, glittering in the light.

"What are you worrying about?" Naliki smiled at him. "It's not your problem. It's certainly not you who's going to be dealing with them. That'll probably be Nkidu." She swung her feet, making the gold and garnet anklets jangle and glitter around her ankles, and grinned wider when Tdroki glared at her. "And besides," she added sweetly, "you don't even want to be king and have responsibility for the kingdom, remember?"

He gritted his teeth, glaring at her furiously and indignantly, and she smirked and gestured in a flippant shrug, jewelry jangling and glittering over her arms, shoulders, breasts. "So just don't think of it as your responsibility." Her grin widened as she goaded him, "And think of it this way: if they end up destroying the kingdom, you won't have to be king! You'll be freed!" She threw her arms up enthusiastically.

He glared at her, silent and furious, and Naliki lowered her arms with a curling smile. "As long as you get out alive, of course."

Tdroki's anger made him seem pretty dense, sometimes—but it was terribly charming in its way.

He was just angry at the world for not being the perfect way he felt it should be.

Tdroki looked away, fists trembling at his sides. There would be pressure marks from the bands of his rings left on the pads of his fingers, he was clenching his hands so hard. "I can't do anything."

He said it like it killed him, and Naliki knew that it did. "I've never been able to do anything! I've never been allowed to do anything!" He whirled on her, looking at her with desperate eyes. "You think I want to be powerless like this?!" He was tensed and trembling.

Naliki didn't mind his anger, but that pained hopelessness was something she wasn't at all okay with, and so she smiled at him mockingly. "And yet you say you don't want to be king. When the king is the most powerful individual in the kingdom."

"That's not power!" Tdroki burst out, gesturing emphatically. His fury was blazing. "The king doesn't do anything! He just tells other people to do things!"

"And then they do," Naliki said, leaning back on her hands and continuing to swing her feet. "And so things get done. Therefore, the king does a lot." She giggled as she had a thought. "It's like having hundreds of thousands of arms! Haven't you ever been frustrated with having only two?" She grinned at him delightedly, throwing out her arms demonstratively. "Think if you had thousands! All the things you'd be able to get done!"

He stared at her with a kind of subdued blankness that probably meant he was either seriously contemplating her point about a king's power or else was trying to imagine her with thousands of arms, and Naliki snorted and set her hands back down on the bed behind her.

"And honestly, Tdroki," she added, looking at him pointedly, "after years of lessons and shadowing our father, you, of all people, should know exactly how much a king does. It's not just sitting on the throne looking pretty." She tilted her head, hair brushing over her shoulder. "You leave the pretty sitting to me, okay?"

Tdroki looked at her and sighed, brushing a hand back through his hair, making it stick straight up instead of all over the place like it had ended up from his tugging on it. He said dryly, "Sitting prettily involves running your mouth, does it?"

Naliki simpered and swung her legs. "Don't even colorful birds sing?"

Tdroki huffed, but he looked a lot more collected; and he was teasing her back, now, which she liked. "You can't call ear-splitting screeches singing."

"One being's scream might be another being's song," she hummed.

It was as much as she could do not to laugh at the indignant way he looked at her.

"First of all," he stated flatly, "that has nothing to do with anything you just said. Second of all"—he looked at her with even more disbelief—"are you trying to say that people's screams are like songs to those monsters? Is that supposed to make me feel better?!" His anger was flaming again, and Naliki smiled.

"Of course not," she said, shaking her head, dark hair brushing over her face. "You don't want to feel better, remember? You want to be angry." She splayed her gold-ringed fingers over the beaded collar-piece draped over her chest and grinned wider. "I have taken it as my responsibility as your dutiful sister to help you feel angry."

Tdroki stared at her like there was a war raging in his head. "...I don't know whether to feel strangely flattered or to tell you to go throw yourself off the roof," he confirmed. He tsked and looked away. "Unlike Luxanthus, you probably wouldn't survive it."

"You probably wouldn't, either," Naliki pointed out fairly. "Nkidu is practically a monster himself, so he's singular like that." She'd watched Nkidu slay the Accursed that the warriors had brought back alive. The monster hadn't even been able to touch him. It had made her wonder how inhuman Nkidu had to be, to be able to kill a monster so easily.

Of course someone like that would survive something as simple as falling off a roof.

"Mm, Tmra might actually survive, too," she mused, meeting Tdroki's burning gaze with a knowing quirk of her lips. "I mean, if he jumped off the roof, he'd probably manage to miss the ground, being the klutz that he is."

Tdroki, ever so protective of them all, and especially the young Tmra, was predictably incensed. "Is that supposed to be funny?"

Naliki smirked at him and kicked her feet. "Didn't I already tell you that I'm trying to make you angry?"

"You don't need to!" Tdroki yelled at her. "I'm already angry!"

"All fires need fuel continually added to them," she pointed out.

The fire of Tdroki's anger lowered to the smolder of red-hot coals. "So you're throwing sticks at me."

She beamed at him. "Basically!"

Tdroki's fists were clenched but he exhaled, closing his eyes. "So I can assume that, no matter how I tell you to go away and leave me alone, you won't." He stated it flatly, resigned and tired.

"Nope!" Naliki agreed, hopping off the bed and crossing lightly over to him, poking him in the side. "I can't let my fire go out. I'd get cold! And it would be so dark!"

Tdroki opened his eyes like searing embers and looked at her bitterly. "Then wait for the sun to rise; Luxanthus is reliable like that."

"If anyone could beat those monsters back, it would be him," Naliki agreed. She wrapped an arm around her older brother's shoulder, pointing up with her other arm. "But the sun is up in the sky, you know." She lowered her hand to poke him in the arm and snickered. "Fire I can coax onto sticks and then jab people in the face with."

Tdroki stared at her disbelievingly. "What, by the Daimmu, is that metaphor supposed to mean?" he muttered, a hand creeping up over his face as he closed his eyes. "Poets, the lot of you." He took a sibilant inhale, opened his eyes, and glared at her through his fingers. "It's exhausting!"

Aww, he was angry again. Naliki grinned at him. "You do it too, you know," she pointed out, poking him again and sniggering. "You're like a puddle complaining that the rain hitting it is wet."

"I hate all of you," he stated flatly.

Naliki wrapped both her arms around his shoulders and buried her face in his neck. "I don't believe you one bit," she informed him.

"Get off," he said.

"No," she replied.

His tone hardened. "I said *get off.*"

"Make me," she said, raising her head to look him in the eye. She grinned at him, sharp and taunting. "Go on, shove me away if you hate me as much as you say. Hit me."

She knew he wouldn't.

Tdroki knew it, too.

His eyes were such blazes that they looked like they should be emitting sparks. "As if I'd do anything you told me to," he sneered at her. "If you want to be hit that badly, then go ahead and hit yourself."

Naliki poked him in the cheek. "Aww, you're acting like a king and telling me to do something instead of doing it yourself."

Tdroki closed his eyes, inhaling and exhaling shakily. He trembled in her embrace. Quietly, bitterly, he said, "You really do make me angry, Naliki."

"I know," she said, leaning in closer to say into his ear: "And you like it." He trembled with all the fury he kept bottled up inside, and she wrapped her arms tighter around him, laying her head on his shoulder. More softly, she said, "I like it, too."

His right hand was clenched in such a tight fist that his entire arm and shoulder were shaking, but his left hand came up to rest gently, innocuously over her waist.

LUXANTHUS'S MUSCLES WERE trembling a little. It had been a full day of training and fighting. Then afterward, he'd stayed out for a couple of hours to practice by himself.

He was maybe a little tired.

He also stank of sweat. He wanted to take a bath with herbs and salts, and then sleep a bit before rising with the sun to begin training again.

At least he was able to fall asleep as soon as his head hit the pillow, now.

He'd finished wiping off his sweat and the layer of dust that had caked to it and was about to head to his chambers when his sister Rkalla appeared, leaning herself against the wall. She was smiling in that way that made her resemble a jackal arrived at a piece of carrion.

"You've really got it hard, huh?" she said, with the honeyed sympathy that always made him feel like she was faking it. Her eyes, a deep red, were keen as any scavenger's. "Everyone's really counting on you, Nkidu. That's got to be a lot of pressure."

Luxanthus nodded. "I need to get better." He needed to become strong and skilled enough to be able to take on multiple Accursed at once, without a single one of them landing a blow against him. He couldn't afford to get killed or infected.

Of course, if he was wounded, he'd kill himself before he could become an Accursed. But that went back to the first point, which was to be able to slay large numbers of Accursed without dying. He knew that he was Ordyuk's best bet for holding back the Accursed. He also knew that because of that, he wouldn't be able to go out and fight them outside of the training arena until he was completely, unequivocally ready.

He couldn't afford to make a mistake or miscalculation and die.

"It doesn't scare you at all?" Rkalla asked.

He admitted truthfully, "Not being strong enough scares me." He met her gaze determinedly. "That's why I'm working on getting stronger. So that I will be strong enough."

Rkalla's lips curved into her jackal smile. "Poor Tdroki beating himself up for his every mistake that lands you with even more intense training, and here you are adding even more on top of that," she said, tilting her head as she regarded him, smile sweet and eyes cunning. "Tdroki isn't making enough mistakes for you, it seems."

Sometimes Luxanthus wanted to find something to place in either side of the braided circlet around the crown of her head to make it look like she had the jackal ears to go with the smile. The way she looked at him like she was evaluating what of his meat was rotten and what of it was still good and could be ripped out with her teeth.

He didn't understand what she was trying to get out of him.

Luxanthus sighed. "What do you want, Rkalla?" he asked.

He was maybe a little tired.

Rkalla pushed off the wall and walked over to him, smiling. "I just wanted to see how my little brother was doing, what with the growing number of those monsters."

"Tmra isn't here." Luxanthus frowned.

That concerned him a little, actually. He hadn't seen his younger brother in a while. Tmra had used to come often to watch him train, but he hadn't done so since shortly after the Accursed had started turning up. Luxanthus wondered if Tmra was okay.

Rkalla rolled her eyes. "I was talking about you, sand-head."

Luxanthus looked down at her, blinking. "...I'm not little," he said.

"But you're still younger than me," she said, crossing her arms beneath her breasts and leaning into a hip. "So you're still my little brother." She said it authoritatively.

"I'm not littler than you, though," Luxanthus pointed out. He gestured between them. "I'm taller and heavier than you." He was already almost as tall as Diyomendon, now, so he certainly must also have been heavier than his older brother due to being more muscular. Diyomendon didn't eat very much. He always said he wasn't hungry.

Luxanthus supposed his older brother hated food as much as he hated the rest of the world.

Rkalla sighed. "You really are boring sometimes, you know?" She looked at him as if it was somehow his fault, and Luxanthus shrugged.

"It's not my duty to be interesting," he pointed out.

Rkalla was all jackal adorned in gold and garnet as she looked at him. "I really don't understand you, Nkidu."

Luxanthus's lips curved. "The feeling is mutual," he assured her. He was maybe a little tired.

Rkalla sighed, her keen scavenger-posture loosening. "Well, I'm glad to see that you're not getting crushed by all the weight that's being placed on you, at least," she said. She turned as if to go.

Luxanthus felt a little guilty. Everyone was counting on him, after all. That included Rkalla.

"The concern is appreciated," he relented. She turned to look back at him, and he held her gaze and imbued his voice with all his confidence, as well as some of the strength that was left in him. "But you may sleep soundly with the reassurance that I will become strong enough to kill those monsters like a hunting dog kills hares."

Rkalla looked at him blankly for a moment and then broke out in a grin. "And then suddenly you're funny!"

Luxanthus pursed his lips. "I was trying to be reassuring," he said, feeling slightly vexed.

Rkalla simpered and patted him on the shoulder. "It's certainly reassuring to know that you have a sense of humor."

Luxanthus was starting to feel undeniably tired.

"I hate to disappoint you," he said, looking down at her and hoping his tiredness wasn't too evident, "but I wasn't actually trying to be funny. I meant what I said." He really had. He might've been a little tired at the moment, but he wanted her to know that she could count on him. He wanted her to believe in him.

He knew that he could do it. It would take some time, but he would get there. He knew that he would.

Rkalla's demeanor softened slightly, so that she no longer

looked so much like a jackal. "I know," she said, patting him again on the shoulder. "And I actually am reassured." She smiled gently, in a way that made Luxanthus think that she actually meant it. "Everyone knows that you'll be able to, Nkidu."

"I won't disappoint you," Luxanthus said earnestly. He let his lips quirk slightly. "Except for in regard to my sense of humor."

Rkalla laughed. "Then stand corrected, because you're not disappointing me there, either." She grinned at him. "Even if the humor is dry." The jackal-glint was back in her eyes, but Luxanthus found that in this instance, he didn't particularly mind.

"Well, you call me 'sand-head' for a reason," he agreed, and Rkalla laughed in a way that seemed genuine. She looked bright and beautiful like that, and Luxanthus felt a bit better than he had before.

"Perhaps 'sand-tongue' would be more accurate," she teased, nudging him in the arm before pushing away, heading back toward the palace. "Well, I'm off now to find my actually little little brother. Don't wear yourself out, Nkidu."

"I won't," Luxanthus promised her. More uncertainly, he added, "I hope you find Tmra okay."

She waved in acknowledgment and disappeared around the corner, dark hair brushing over her bead-net-adorned shoulders.

Luxanthus looked down and sighed. He picked up the dirtied cloth he'd been wiping himself off with and headed toward his chambers, barely able to think of more than drawing himself a warm bath to clean the sweat and grime from his skin and relax his aching muscles, and then lying down in bed and closing his eyes, letting sleep carry him like a boat floating on the Aru River.

He was maybe more than a little tired.

SOMETIMES REZEKYRIOS FELT like he broke everything he touched.

He was so clumsy and uncoordinated, his limbs feeling like

they hardly belonged to him, and sometimes he could barely even see anything with how much his eyes hurt. And so he fumbled, and he stumbled, and he dropped things, tripped over them, or crashed right into them.

The glass sculpture was on the floor in shattered pieces, and panic swelled in Rezekyrios's chest like the rainy season brought the Aru River to flood its banks.

"Aww," came Naliki's whining voice, "that was my favorite ugly glass sculpture."

"I…" Rezekyrios could barely get words out past the panic welling from his chest to fill his throat, drown his tongue, push insistently at the backs of his eyes. "I'm sorry…"

"I was joking!" said Naliki, too loudly, and Rezekyrios flinched. She was hovering over him. He could hardly see. He didn't know what her expression looked like. "Seriously, good for you for finally knocking over the thing! Now they'll have to replace it, and hopefully the next one won't be so ugly!"

Rezekyrios chewed on his lower lip. It hurt.

"Hey, hey." Her hands on his shoulders. "Stop that now. It'll bleed."

Rezekyrios stopped chewing his lip, gritting his teeth together instead. He looked down because he couldn't meet her gaze. He couldn't. "I'm sorry."

"You don't have to apologize," she said, and Rezekyrios felt wretched.

"I'm…" He couldn't find the words. His thoughts were as scattered and sharp as the shattered glass on the ground.

If he walked over those shards, he'd cut open the bottoms of his feet. He kind of wanted to.

"Seriously, what's with you?" Naliki was asking. She sounded reproachful, and there was panic in Rezekyrios like flooding water, like blistering heat, and he could hardly think. Naliki's hands were still on his shoulders. He wanted to pull away. "You're so jumpy,

Tmra. We're not monsters. We're not going to eat your flesh or drink your blood."

Sometimes he felt like she wanted to.

She was speaking quickly. "And I mean, yeah, there are monsters out there that would try to, but they're far away!"

Rezekyrios's eyes hurt. He wanted to rub them. He couldn't, because his sister's hands were on his shoulders. Also, she'd tell him to stop, like she'd told him to stop chewing his lip.

If he didn't do either of those things, he'd have to do something else. He had to do something. If they didn't want him to do those things, then what was he supposed to do?

He was going to suffocate in the mounting sandstorm of panic, fall apart to dust beneath its terrible touch.

Naliki cursed, and Rezekyrios flinched. "I just made this worse, didn't I?" she said. She sounded distressed, and the panic in Rezekyrios was disintegrating him from the inside out.

Naliki's grip loosened. It would've been better if she'd tightened it. That would have grounded him. He was crumbling away.

"Hanging out with Tdroki so much might not be the best idea," his sister was saying. "He's bad for my ability to be gentle."

"But you don't break things." The words fell like glass shards from Rezekyrios's tongue.

"What?" said Naliki.

All of Rezekyrios's thoughts were shattered like glass and hurting him. He struggled with them, managed to say disjointedly, "The way you move. It's gentle. You don't break things. I—" Thoughts and feelings in his head like so many sharp fragments, and he thought that walking over the ones on the ground would have hurt less. That the pain of bleeding feet would have been a relief in comparison.

He was tense and shaking, and he felt dimly that he was smiling, his face having simply ended up that way from the anxiety drawing taut his muscles. "—I always break everything."

"Hey, it's—" Naliki started.

Rezekyrios wasn't supposed to interrupt other people; he did so anyway. "Why aren't I punished for it?"

"What?" asked Naliki.

"When Diyomendon and Nkidu make mistakes, they're punished for them," Rezekyrios said. The glass shards in his mind were slicing his tongue open, now. "Even if Diyomendon's punishment is Nkidu being punished, they're both punished. And you too, Rkalla—even you are told off when you do something wrong or do something you're not supposed to." Rezekyrios looked everywhere except for at her face. Everywhere except for her eyes, deep-dark red, like blood. "Why is it then when I make mistakes, no one ever says anything? Why am I never punished?" He couldn't look her in the eyes. He couldn't.

"Um…" Naliki couldn't seem to think of anything to say.

Rezekyrios was smiling, but not from anything like happiness. "It's because I'm hopeless, isn't it?" he said. The shattered pieces of his thoughts were falling like rain, now, scattering like expanding ripples over the floor and drawing blood on their way. "There's no point in correcting me when I'll never be able to do anything correctly. Everyone's given up on me, and so you all just tell me it's okay." His voice—like glass—cracked. "Because I can't help it."

"Hey, Tmra," Naliki said, "look, it's…" She trailed off, stopping whatever she was about to say.

Rezekyrios could guess what it was, and he looked up at her and smiled like a reflection in a cracked mirror smiled. "It's okay?"

His eyes were aching painfully, but he could make out the stunned and shaken expression on Naliki's face. He shook his head as if he could clear the image from his mind, but it stayed.

"I'm sorry—" he started, and then caught himself. "No, you told me not to say sorry. I'm…" If he couldn't say sorry, then what else was there? He had no other words. He had no other feelings.

He was just sorry, but he wasn't allowed to say it.

"I have nothing to say," was all he could manage, before pulling out of his sister's grasp to get away, find somewhere to hide, curl up somewhere where nobody would stumble on him, where he couldn't break anything, where he could count seconds until his heartbeat calmed and he could breathe normally again.

"Tmra!" Naliki called after him. "You should at least go see Nkidu sometime! He can't look for you since he's so busy now, but he misses you, you know!"

Rezekyrios turned a corner and kept running.

He couldn't see Nkidu. Not now.

Not when Nkidu was working so hard to be able to protect the kingdom, while Rezekyrios wasn't able to do anything but break things.

YTHIRIS HAD BEEN YOUNG at the time of the Great Calamity, and she didn't remember much about it. What she did remember, though, was burned into her memory.

She remembered the dawn breaking, and with it a great, crawling tide from the desert, flowing over the southern wall of the city. She remembered the screams, the blood that had run through the streets and soaked into the mudbrick. She remembered the panic, remembered her father, the king's most trusted adviser—like her brother now was to her husband—shouting orders, remembered him ushering her into the palace with the other noble children and women.

She remembered crying, until the former queen and high priestess had stroked her hair and told her to pray to the Daimmu: to tell them the things she loved about Ordyuk and the world the Daimmu had created, the things she was grateful for and wanted to see another day. The former queen had smiled at her slyly, and told her that the Daimmu were finicky, arrogant beings, and they were flattered when they and their work were praised.

"Don't think about your fears when you pray to the Daimmu,"

the former queen had told her. "Think only of your gratitude, and of your hopes and dreams for the future."

And so Ythiris had prayed. She'd thought of the colorful sunrises and sunsets that took her breath away; she'd thought of the sun and its warmth, the moon and its soft light; she'd thought of the life-giving River Aru, of the fleets of boats it carried and the crops that grew so well along its fertile banks; she thought of the golden sands and the beautiful glass sculptures that could be created from it; she thought of the hearth fires, of the way the companionable flames drove away the dark and cold of night; she thought of pomegranate fruits, and of breads and cakes sweetened with honey and dates; she thought of the bustling city full of life, of her mother and father and little brother; she thought of their dog and their cats, and of the corpses of the venomous snakes the felines brought back.

She'd thought of what she wanted for the future. She imagined becoming queen and high priestess; imagined watching Ordyuk flourish and getting to participate in the royal dances to honor the deities; imagined having children of her own to cherish and watch grow.

I'm so grateful for this life I've had, she'd thought, *I want to keep living it.* She thought to the Daimmu: *The world you've created is beautiful; I want to keep living in it.*

She'd felt a warmth in her mind, then. Had felt presences outside of her own, and had felt assured and calmed.

One of the women had started humming. A few others had joined in. Ythiris had started clapping her hands and stomping her feet. Other children had joined in.

Soon the women were singing, and the children were clapping and stomping along with the beat. Then someone started dancing—maybe it was Ythiris, maybe it was someone else—and then they were all dancing. Dancing and singing and imagining the delight of seeing another beautiful dawn, imagining the continued glory of the country they held so close in their hearts.

By the end of the Great Calamity, Ordyuk had been devastated. But according to the news they'd receive from travelers over the years, Ordyuk had fared far better than the kingdoms to the west and the north.

The people of Ordyuk had always known they were favored by the Daimmu.

Even with the reappearance of the Accursed, that faith did not waver. They prayed in gratitude for the lives they had lived, prayed for the future of Ordyuk, for the future of their children and their children's children.

Even though the Accursed had returned, the Daimmu were on their side and would aid them, like they'd always been and had always done.

AT THE TIME OF THE Great Calamity, the adults had tried to usher the young Agamenjiyr deeper into the castle with the other noble children. Agamenjiyr had refused.

He'd gone up to the top of the palace roof, and had watched as Ordyuk crawled with monsters, flowed with blood, and echoed with screams.

His father the king had been a great warrior, and had gone out with the rest of the Ordyukian Army that wasn't protecting the palace to exterminate the monsters in the city and defend the people. Agamenjiyr had known that he might not come back. If his father didn't come back, he would be the next king.

As the next king, his Ordyuk would be one ravaged by the Accursed. If he was to rule that kingdom, he wanted to witness exactly what it went through, however terrible. It was going to be his kingdom. He would not hide from it. He would not be able to banish a darkness that he did not understand.

And so he stood on the roof and watched, with tears tracking black kohl down his cheeks like the facial markings of a cheetah, a great heaviness settling on his shoulders like the sky itself was using him as its pillar.

Even as the city was filled with blood and screams, Agamenjiyr stood on the roof and watched with his back straight and his legs steady, so that the sky that was leaning on him would not fall.

Since that day, he'd never stopped carrying that weight.

WHEN DIYOMENDON WENT up to the palace roof in the cover of night, he found Luxanthus sitting on the edge with his legs dangling over.

It was far from the first time Diyomendon had found him up there, and it wasn't likely to be the last.

Luxanthus looked like he'd come to the roof straight from training, his leanly muscled torso covered with a thin layer of sweat-streaked dust, his hair slightly mussed in a way it never was other-wise, his jewelry restricted to a few gold bangles around his wrists and ankles. He was still wearing his leather sandals.

Diyomendon, barefoot, sat down cross-legged next to him but not completely beside him. He huffed an exhale. "A full day of train-ing, and you still have the energy to come up here?"

Luxanthus didn't bother looking over at him. "I didn't practice as long by myself afterward," he said, keeping his gaze on the sleep-ing city. "Relaxation is important, too. I don't want to forget what I'm fighting for." His tone was mild and inflectionless, which was typical of him. "I don't want to lose sight of myself."

Diyomendon never spoke without inflection. "What are you fighting for?" he asked his younger brother, looking over at him.

The young warrior looked out over Ordyuk. His eyes that were sunlight-gold in the sunlight were moonlight-silver in the moonlight. Which was about what could be expected from someone as undeni-ably blessed by the Daimmu as Luxanthus. The thick outlines of black kohl around his eyes made his irises look all the brighter.

After a while of contemplative silence, during which only the wind whispered between them, the Daimmu-Blessed answered, "Moments like this, I suppose." He looked over at Diyomendon with his placid gaze. "Things like the city being peaceful at night, and you not being so angry."

The thing about Luxanthus was that he was always absolutely earnest, and Diyomendon let out an exhale that could only be inelegantly described as an ill-bred cross between a sigh, a groan, and a hiss. "I hate you, Luxanthus." He glared at the space of roof between his knees and the edge and jabbed it hard with a finger. "But it's incredibly difficult to be angry at you."

The younger boy hummed beside him. "I'm glad of that, at least. I'd rather you not be angry at me."

Luxanthus was so completely earnest, in absolutely everything he did and said, and Diyomendon jabbed harder at the roof and imagined being able to burn dark marks into it.

It was unfair. What with the shadow-faceless, shadow-untouchable demeanor the young warrior usually exhibited on top of his physical perfection, it could make a person wonder if he was even human and if he even felt anything at all.

Diyomendon knew full well that he did, though, which made him hate it all the more.

"How do you do it?" he asked bitterly, jabbing at the roof.

"Do what?" Luxanthus asked mildly.

"Carry everyone's expectations for you and just accept it," Diyomendon sneered, lifting his gaze and looking over at his brother with his anger feeling hot and overwhelming inside of him. "Why, by the Daimmu, aren't you angry?"

Luxanthus blinked back at him, looking, as always, utterly unperturbed. "I don't see anything to be angry about," he said simply. Completely earnestly.

Diyomendon gritted his teeth so hard his jaw ached, and Luxanthus tilted his head, gazing back at him impassively. "Why does it make you so angry, Diyomendon?"

The force of Diyomendon's indignant fury drove him to his feet. "Because they're trying to force us to be certain things," he said heatedly. "To be a certain way. To do certain things. To feel certain things." He was aware that he'd started pacing and gesticulating, but he didn't care. It was just Luxanthus there, and Luxanthus certainly didn't care either. "They expect certain things from you, expect you to be certain things, and if you don't fulfill their expectations, then you're wrong! Everything you are is *wrong.*" He whirled on his younger brother, feeling like he looked wild. "How does it not infuriate you?!"

Luxanthus looked back at him, utterly unmoved, and then turned his gaze away and shrugged. "Maybe I'm exactly what people expect of me," he suggested mildly. The Daimmu-Blessed gazed out over Ordyuk, and Diyomendon sighed, his anger evaporating as he sat down next to the younger boy again.

It was impossible to be angry at Luxanthus.

"If I push you off the roof and tell you that I expect you to live, will you?" Diyomendon asked him flatly.

Luxanthus glanced over at him. "I will endeavor my utmost to do so," he answered.

"Why?" Diyomendon demanded, looking at him aslant.

Luxanthus blinked at him. "Because I don't want to die?" he offered, as if the answer were so obvious that he was confused why the question had even been asked.

Diyomendon snorted, looking away. "Fair enough." He jabbed unheedingly at the mudbrick. "I'm not going to push you off the roof," he added, after a moment.

Luxanthus snorted lightly beside him. "You wouldn't be able to, even if you truly wanted to," he pointed out.

They both knew that Luxanthus was far stronger physically, and the differences in their musculature would have left no doubt of that fact in anyone's mind.

"I could order you to jump off the roof," Diyomendon said.

Pure physical strength wasn't the only kind of power. As his sister so often liked to tauntingly remind him.

There was a slight tilt to Luxanthus's lips. "I wouldn't have to obey, you know. You're not king yet." He looked over at Diyomendon again, and he actually appeared amused. "Once you're king, then you can order me to jump off the roof."

And people thought the young warrior had no sense of humor.

Probably because even when he made his wisecracks, he was also being completely, utterly earnest.

Diyomendon looked away. "I'd have to be a real idiot of a king to do that," he pointed out. He jabbed vaguely at the mudbrick. He wished it would burn.

"I'm not the only one whose training has intensified," Luxanthus remarked softly.

Diyomendon snorted. "I don't think you can exactly draw a comparison," he said acridly, jabbing at the roof some more.

"True," Luxanthus said mildly, looking away finally, turning his gaze out over Ordyuk. "Dealing with the kingdom's bureaucracy looks much more exhausting."

"Pfft." Diyomendon couldn't help the incredulous grin that stretched across his face as he glanced over at his younger brother. "I would say that fighting all day and training to slay monsters would be far worse, but you actually sounded like you meant that."

Luxanthus met his gaze easily. "I did," he said. Completely, utterly earnest.

Diyomendon let out some kind of ungainly hybrid of a huff and a groan, falling forward over his crossed legs so that his head almost touched the ground. "Stop giving people reasons to believe you're an idiot," he muttered.

"I wouldn't equate honesty or simplicity with idiocy," came Luxanthus's mild reply. There was still a note of amusement in his voice. "Oftentimes, the idiot is the one who makes things more complicated than necessary."

Diyomendon straightened up and glared at him, feeling a stirring of anger in his gut that didn't quite want to ignite. "Are you calling me an idiot and saying that I make things too complicated?"

"No," Luxanthus said, holding his gaze with an expression that was utterly mild except for his twitching lips, "but that was an idiotic question that unnecessarily complicated what I was trying to say."

Diyomendon tried to stir the embers of anger in his gut into a flame, quickly realized it was in vain, and gave up.

"I can't even get angry at you," he muttered darkly, jabbing at the roof. "I hate you." More jabbing.

No matter how hard he jabbed at the mudbrick, he'd never leave burn marks.

"Why do you hate me for not making you angry?" Luxanthus inquired, utterly mild. Earnestly asking. Diyomendon couldn't even get angry at him for it.

"Things would be so much easier if I could be angry at you," he muttered, jabbing at the roof. He imagined scorch marks. Dark, black scorch marks.

Luxanthus pointed out mildly, "But you'd also hate me if I did make you angry."

Diyomendon jabbed at the ground and imagined the black scorch marks he wanted to leave there curling with smoke. "So?"

"So then you'd hate me either way," Luxanthus recapitulated. Still completely, earnestly mild.

Diyomendon kept jabbing imagined scorch marks into the mudbrick. "So what?"

The younger boy exhaled softly. If it was a sigh, it wasn't one of exasperation, but of acceptance. "Okay," Luxanthus said. "I'll content myself with this, then." There were the faintest traces of a smile on his lips when Diyomendon looked over at him, the younger boy gazing easily out over the dark city, or perhaps the dark horizon past it. "If you're going to hate me whether or not you're angry at me, I prefer that you hate me without also being angry."

Diyomendon snorted. "You're unbelievable," he said, with feeling.

Luxanthus's lips twitched as he glanced over to meet his gaze. "That is the general expectation that people have of me, yes."

Diyomendon actually laughed. Not a snicker or a huff, but a full laugh.

If that wasn't miracle enough, or a sign that the world was possibly ending, Luxanthus then made an expression that indicated surprise. Diyomendon could not remember a single instance of having ever seen the Daimmu-Blessed look surprised by anything.

In all honesty, though, the laugh had surprised Diyomendon, too.

"You have a nice laugh," Luxanthus informed him, after Diyomendon had stopped. The younger boy was watching him with an indecipherable expression.

Diyomendon glared at him and gritted his teeth so hard and fast that his upper and lower canines caught against each other, creating an unpleasant grating sensation that almost made him flinch as he bit out, "So what?"

Luxanthus looked at him with that quiet expression and said, completely earnestly, "I'd fight any number of monsters for a world where I got to hear it more."

The curl of his lips that Diyomendon gave him was some monstrous fusion of an amused grin and a disparaging sneer. "Then don't bother. You could slay all the monsters in the world and that still wouldn't happen."

Luxanthus blinked at him. "I don't need to kill all the monsters in the world," the Daimmu-Blessed said mildly, tilting his head, gaze steady and utterly assured. "I just need to not die while taking on the ones that I do fight."

Diyomendon snorted. "Way to be unambitious," he said, lips

curling wryly.

The younger boy shrugged. "Well, I'm certainly not trying to become the king," he pointed out. Completely earnestly.

Diyomendon knew he hadn't meant anything by it, but it still set his teeth on edge. "I'm *not* trying to become king," he said, low and dark. Smoldering coals on his tongue and behind his eyes, glowing red-hot in his mind. "I'm not *trying* to become king."

"You're simply becoming one," Luxanthus surmised, regarding him mildly. "Because that's what you are."

"It's what I'm being made to be." Diyomendon spat the words out like ash.

Luxanthus looked at him easily, utterly phlegmatic, and said, "Way to be unambitious."

Diyomendon let out a surprised laugh. Again. For the second time that night. He could now count the number of times he could remember laughing like that on two fingers instead of just one. "I hate you," he told his younger brother once the laugh and its aftershocks had faded.

"I know," Luxanthus said, looking out into the dark with a slight curve to his lips.

Diyomendon huffed quietly. Following his younger brother's gaze, he looked out over the Kingdom of Ordyuk that would one day be his. The two of them remained silent.

The night-serenade of insects that had once seemed calming now carried with it a hint of threat.

"I should probably get some rest," Luxanthus said eventually, pushing himself to his feet.

"You should," Diyomendon agreed.

The Daimmu-Blessed didn't tell him that he should do the same, simply taking his leave.

Diyomendon went back inside once he got tired of imagining Ordyuk burning.

III

THE WAY NKIDU FOUGHT, if the ground had been covered in hot coals and he'd been barefoot, he would have taken out all his opponents before burning his feet.

Naliki watched him dodge the spidery appendages of an Accursed more easily than a child playing jump-rope or a dancer crashing a casual game of amateur limbo, and then sweep in for the kill with such speed that Naliki barely saw what was happening before the Accursed's severed head was rolling over the packed dirt and Nkidu was flipping out of the way of the giant spider appendages' death throes.

The monster's body went finally still as Nkidu walked out of the training arena, pulling off the thin cowl that Bardyuk-style warriors used to shield their mouths, noses, and sometimes also eyes from the dust and sand they kicked up. He used the cloth to wipe the sweat from his face and neck—which was probably the garment's secondary use, all things considered.

Naliki met him with a smile. "Looking monstrous out there, Nkidu," she said.

Her younger brother looked at her a bit petulantly. He didn't say anything about her calling him monstrous, though, stating only, "They still won't let me fight more than one at once."

He sounded about as displeased as she'd ever heard him, and she hummed. "Can you blame them for not wanting to risk your dying?"

Nkidu looked at her blandly. "They expect me to be the one to defend the kingdom from the Accursed and then won't let me fight them?" He was definitely resentful.

"You're a growing boy, and they're not that desperate yet," Naliki told him, puffing a breath over her lips. "If things get really bad, you can bet they'll shove you out there." Despite his being only fourteen and an entire year younger than she was, he was already almost a head taller, and she had to look up at him.

It was great, though, that he was already as tall and strong as he was, because sometimes when they got caught in crowds, he would carry her on his shoulders so that she could see above everyone.

Of course, that was usually only so that they could find Tmra, who had a tendency to get separated from them and end up lost.

Nkidu looked like he was thinking about saying something else, but ended up changing his mind and altering the subject, settling for, "How's Tmra?"

They were all concerned about their youngest sibling.

It was hard not to be.

Naliki forced a smile. "He's doing about as well as could be expected."

Nkidu looked at her. "Which means?"

Naliki had to fight not to roll her eyes. For someone whose irises were like sunlight, Nkidu really wasn't very bright, sometimes.

"He's not doing that great, genius." She didn't like having to say it. Having to say it made it hurt worse. She didn't understand why Nkidu always forced people to say things that should have been understood without needing to be said.

"I see," the boy said, looking away.

"But how about you?" Naliki changed the subject, giving him a smile. "How is it fighting those monsters?" It was a safer topic than Tmra, and she was curious.

Nkidu also relaxed slightly, more comfortable with talk of fighting than talk of emotions. "The way they move is different, and it depends on the kinds of appendages they have. But their movement and attack styles reflect those of the arachnids they resemble, which is helpful." He looked back at the training arena and the pieces of the monster's corpse that were being cleared away, then back at her. "It's nothing I can't get used to."

"Are they as strong as they say?" she wondered.

"Their strength doesn't matter if you don't let them touch you," Nkidu said. "It's their speed that's more of a problem." He held her gaze. "It just means that I need to train my reflexes."

He said it perfectly straightforwardly and analytically, and Naliki wasn't quite sure whether to feel assured or disturbed and concerned. "You're so serious," she remarked, smiling.

Nkidu looked at her soberly. "I'd die if I took this lightly. And then even more people would die."

"True," Naliki relented, keeping the blithe rictus on her face.

Nkidu looked at her for another few moments and then sighed, closing his eyes. "What do you want, Rkalla?" he asked, tone flat.

Every time she talked with him, he asked her that.

It hurt, but Naliki acted as if it didn't. "Is it so disagreeable for your older sister to want to check up on you?" she asked, and pouted a bit.

Nkidu looked at her in a way that could only have been described as jaded. "You have a rather obfuscated way of doing so," he said flatly.

Naliki rocked on her feet. "The best path between two points isn't always a straight line," she hummed. Her lips curved teasingly but she watched him carefully.

He blinked at her, and she saw the sudden moment of compre-hension in his gaze. "It would depend on the terrain, yes," he said, as if everything now made sense.

Naliki wasn't sure if he understood what she meant by it meta-phorically or if he was only thinking about it literally, but she still felt uplifted at his typical-Nkidu response and typical-Nkidu reac-tion. "I'm glad to see you're doing okay," she said, meaning it.

"What about you?" Nkidu asked, looking at her with much more gentleness than before. "How are you, Rkalla?"

She smiled at him, feeling pleased but also vindictive. "About as well as could be expected."

The boy's gaze closed off so fast it was either sad or comical. His voice was tired again as he asked dully, "Which means?"

Naliki maybe felt a little bad for messing with him like that, but also she honestly didn't know how to answer the question. "The usual." She shrugged, carefully light. "I'm doing better than Tdroki and Tmra, but none of us are ever doing so well as you."

Nkidu sighed. "You really avoid saying anything in a way that's pellucid, don't you." It was phrased like a question but lacked the intonation of one.

Naliki couldn't help but grin. "I'm pretty sure that talking to me is the only time you ever show your exhaustion," she needled him, grinning wider as he looked at her long-sufferingly.

"And what do you get from seeing me like this?" he asked, tone and gaze dull. She felt much better about life, seeing him like that. If dealing with her was the most exhausting thing in his life, and she was only even able to bother him this much, then there wasn't any-thing to worry about. Ordyuk would be fine.

Naliki simpered and wiggled her fingers at him. "I'm just disturbing rocks to try to catch glimpses of the scorpions and other creepy-crawlies that hide underneath them."

If she asked questions straight out, all she'd ever get from people were the lies they wanted her to see. The lies that everything was okay. She needed to annoy people and get under their skin in order to see what feelings were actually lying beneath the surface. How much people were actually hurting; what fears were bothering them.

Nkidu looked at her tiredly, but not altogether without comprehension. "And what do you get from seeing them, Rkalla?"

The kind of funny thing about Nkidu was that he seemed to understand representational metaphors more clearly than plain speech. It made some things harder, but some things easier.

"Well, when I see them then I know what I need to watch out for," Naliki explained. "If I need to watch out for scorpions or spiders or snakes. How many of them there are; how big they are." She shrugged lightly, smiling. "You can't do anything about them unless you drive them out, you know?"

Nkidu blinked, gaze going distant and contemplative. "'Drive them out,' huh," he murmured, seemingly to himself. He met her eyes again. "I think I understand what you're saying." His stare was steady and confident. "But you don't need to worry about anything like that with me."

If there was anyone who wouldn't be crushed by the weight of any fears or doubts, it would be Nkidu.

Naliki smiled. "For the sake of everyone in Ordyuk," she said, eyeing him with open dubiety, "I hope that's true." She was still testing him.

Nkidu snorted. "Well, you certainly aren't helping," he muttered pointedly, almost pettishly, and Naliki laughed, genuinely delighted at the peevish reaction. If that was the extent of his reaction even when she prodded, there really was nothing to worry about.

"Okay, okay," she relented, smiling more softly. "I'll leave you alone now." The relief in his gaze was almost comical, and so as she was leaving, she couldn't help but call back, "Don't let the creepy-crawlies get to you, Nkidu!"

She meant both the Accursed as well as any doubts or fears in his head, and she wasn't sure which of those intended meanings he understood her to have meant, but she left laughing with the memory of his endearingly disgruntled expression lingering in her mind.

She genuinely hoped that was the most distressed she'd ever see him.

FOR ALL THAT OTHERS perceived Luxanthus as being stolid and self-possessed, he was actually incredibly impatient.

There was a much larger gap between his abilities and their expectations of him than he figured anyone realized, and he wanted to bridge it as quickly as possible.

And yet they were also underestimating him and holding him back. They told him they were counting on him to defend the kingdom from the Accursed, but then they wouldn't let him fight the monsters. They were contradicting themselves, and it confused and distressed him.

"We can't afford to let you fight the Accursed outside of the training arena until you're absolutely ready," they told him, but when would they deem him 'ready'?

"I'm ready now," he told them, but they shook their heads.

"Not yet," they told him.

"Then when?" he asked, but they could do nothing but shake their heads.

"Not yet."

"Then how will you know when?" He felt frustrated and angry like he'd never felt in his life. He couldn't help but think of his sister's words: that they wouldn't let him fight until they were too desperate to be able to avoid it.

"If you wait until you don't have a choice but to risk my potential death—which won't happen, by the way—then it might be too late," he told them.

One of the warriors took pity on him, clapping him on the shoulder. "Can you blame us for not wanting to risk your life until it's absolutely necessary to do so?" the man asked.

Luxanthus could only look down, an unfamiliar twisting in his stomach. He wasn't used to these feelings. "I'm ready," he said quietly, gaze on the ground. "You know that I'm ready. I'm already better than the rest of you." He knew that it was true. He knew that they had to know that it was true.

The sympathetic soldier chuckled at him. "Yes," the man said, "but we're more expendable than you. There have been Accursed attacks, yes, but it's not yet an emergency situation. We can handle it for the time being.

"Keep training so that when you finally go out there—if it turns out we need you to, which, by the Daimmu, we are hoping it won't— none of them will have a single chance against you."

Luxanthus understood. He did. But it was still frustrating.

"It hurts that there are warriors dying," he said, "when, if I was out there, I could prevent that from happening."

The man clapped him on the shoulder and laughed jovially. "Every man who becomes a soldier is prepared and willing to give up his life."

"But it's not necessary that you all do so," Luxanthus said.

The way the man suddenly looked at him made Luxanthus's gut twist.

"I don't know what your reasons for fighting are, Prince Luxanthus," the warrior said. "But the rest of us aren't doing this because it's necessary for us to do so. We're doing this because we want to."

Luxanthus looked up at him, at a sudden loss of what to say, and the warrior smiled at him in a way that looked like some kind of sadness, clapped him once more on the shoulder, and turned to go.

"Keep training, Prince Luxanthus. And maybe take some time to think about why you're really doing this."

"Does it matter?" Luxanthus asked quietly. "If it's necessary and I don't have a choice in the first place, then my only choices are to either accept it and feel that I want it, or else to hate it." Like his older brother.

The older warrior stopped. "Well, when you put it that way..."

"I want to help you," Luxanthus stated, firmly. "If you also want to be doing what you're doing, then you have to understand that."

The warrior's expression softened sympathetically. "I understand your viewpoint," he said. "But you have to understand ours, too, and why we can't allow you to fight the Accursed outside of the training arena just yet."

There was a frustration in Luxanthus like he'd never known, but he did understand. He hated it, but he understood.

Perhaps this was how his older brother felt all the time.

"I will train my utmost to be able to help when—if—the time comes," he said, and meant it.

"That's the warrior's spirit," the older warrior said. Then, more quietly, he added, "It hurts us too, you know. The fact that we can't save everyone." He straightened his shoulders, and said more loudly and firmly, "But we save those we can. And that's worth it."

Luxanthus felt like a rain cloud full of water that was refused the right to fall, but he lifted his chin, straightened his shoulders, and nodded.

It was difficult to reconcile the fact that people had both overwhelmingly inhuman and underwhelmingly human expectations of him, but he would endeavor his utmost to be everything that was required of him. It was what was necessary, and so it was also what he wanted.

There was, for him, no difference between those two things. There never had been.

REZEKYRIOS RAN INTO Nkidu completely on accident. Literally: he literally ran into him in the hallway, and it was an accident.

Nkidu caught him.

"Whoa," Nkidu said, steadying him with a strong hand and a kind tone. "Careful."

Rezekyrios bit hard on his lip. "I'm sorry." He hadn't meant to. He should've been looking where he was going. He should've been thinking.

He couldn't think. He couldn't seem to be able to think. His mind was so many disconnected shards of shattered glass reflecting completely different parts of the sky. He felt that some of the pieces had been kicked into yesterday, and some into tomorrow, such that he couldn't be sure what was happening, what had already happened, and what he was imagining could happen but might not.

"For what?" Nkidu asked him gently. Unlike Naliki, who always seemed to want to suck him dry of blood, and Diyomendon, who always seemed to want to burn him alive, Nkidu was always gentle. Rezekyrios felt awful.

"For running into you?" he said, confused at why it came out uncertain and intoned like a question.

"It didn't hurt me," Nkidu said, without any bitterness or anger at all. He was looking at Rezekyrios with such kind concern and Rezekyrios felt awful. "Are you hurt?"

Rezekyrios shook his head. "No. I'm fine." Nkidu was doing so much already. He was training so he could defend the kingdom. Rezekyrios couldn't add on to his troubles. He was useless to do anything, so he should at least try to refrain from being a burden.

He chewed on his lip. Unlike Naliki or Diyomendon, Nkidu wouldn't tell him to stop, and Rezekyrios was grateful because he didn't know what else he could do to keep from falling apart. "And I'm..." The words were blocked in his head, in his throat, but Nkidu was looking at him with such kind eyes, and he felt awful for being so incompetent. At the bare minimum he could force out a few words, and so he forced out, however disjointedly, "I'm still sorry. Maybe not for that, but. Something else."

Why were words so difficult? Thoughts. Why were they so difficult? Scattered all over the place in shards that he couldn't seem to piece together.

"What is it?" said Nkidu. Kindly. He was so kind it hurt. Rezekyrios felt awful.

"I was avoiding you," he managed to get out. He couldn't meet his brother's gaze.

Terrible silence for a moment, and then Nkidu asked softly, "Did I do something?" The pain in his voice hurt Rezekyrios, and the younger boy shook his head vehemently.

"No!" he said hurriedly. It wasn't Nkidu's fault. Nkidu hadn't done anything.

It was all him. It was all Rezekyrios.

Another terrible pause, and then Nkidu said, "Did I not do something?" and he sounded so wounded, and Rezekyrios felt so wretched.

"No!" he insisted. He didn't want Nkidu to feel terrible. It wasn't Nkidu's fault—nothing was Nkidu's fault—and he was already doing so much. Rezekyrios couldn't be a burden to him. "I just..." Words. They were so hard. But he couldn't leave Nkidu feeling bad. Nothing was Nkidu's fault. Nkidu was the best.

Rezekyrios couldn't do much, but he could at least force a few words out.

"I feel bad," he blurted. There was so much pain and panic and he could hardly think, but for Nkidu—for Nkidu's sake, at least, he had to. "You're the one who's going to have to fight all those monsters, and I can't do anything." The words came tumbling out, cutting him bloody. "I can't do anything at all."

As long as it wasn't Nkidu who was hurting. Rezekyrios wasn't necessary, so it didn't matter if he hurt; he didn't want to hurt Nkidu, though. He'd be worse than useless if he hurt Nkidu.

Nkidu wrapped his arms around him, pulling him close. He was so comfortingly warm and Rezekyrios's eyes stung.

"You do help me," Nkidu told him. "You give me hope."

Rezekyrios could tell that his brother meant it, but he could only shake his head, feeling utterly wretched. "Not like this I don't," he said, the words tumbling out. "I'm making you comfort me." It hurt so terribly.

"You're not making me do anything," Nkidu said softly, still holding him close. He was so warm. "I do what I want to." Nkidu's thumb brushed over his cheek, Nkidu's gold eyes in his vision and it was simultaneously all Rezekyrios could see and yet he couldn't really see it at all. The panic in his head and chest was so loud.

"I'd kill as many monsters as it took to see you smile again," Nkidu told him softly, and Rezekyrios knew it was true and it made him feel like he was disintegrating.

"You shouldn't have to kill monsters to see me smile," he said, shaking his head. That wasn't fair to Nkidu.

"Yes, that smile is exactly what I'm fighting for," Nkidu said, thumb brushing over his cheek beneath his eye. "So that I'll be able to see it time and time again."

Rezekyrios hadn't even realized he was smiling, and he felt horrible because he wasn't even smiling from happiness, but because everything hurt and he felt so wretched and his face had just somehow ended up that way.

"What if I can't smile one day, though?" he said, and he could barely manage the words, and yet they were tumbling out. "And it's not your fault?"

He was dizzy, his eyes hurt, he could barely breathe, and he could barely see. And it was all him—none of it was Nkidu's fault. Nkidu shouldn't have to feel bad because of him.

Nkidu's touch was so gentle, and his voice, too. "Is something the matter, Tmra?" He sounded so desolate that Rezekyrios wanted to cry.

He couldn't cry, though. He was already so weak, he couldn't cry on top of everything else.

"I just…" Nkidu was looking at him, but Rezekyrios couldn't meet his gaze, looking everywhere around him except for Nkidu's face, Nkidu's eyes. He felt so utterly helpless, so utterly pathetic. "I just want to be able to help," he said, but he couldn't do anything.

"You're not the only one who feels like that, Rezekyrios."

It wasn't Nkidu's voice that answered, but Diyomendon's, and Rezekyrios tensed.

Diyomendon's voice was searing like flame, burning him.

"Everyone is feeling like that," Diyomendon's fierce voice said, the words searing themselves into Rezekyrios's mind and skin. "Except for Luxanthus there. He feels fine. The rest of us feel awful, though."

Diyomendon's hand on his shoulder, pulling him from Nkidu's grasp, and Rezekyrios always felt like Diyomendon should be burning to the touch but he never was. Nkidu let him go so as not to hurt him, and Diyomendon gripped his wrist and pulled him away. "Come on, Luxanthus has work to do. Let's not hold him back with our uselessness."

Diyomendon's words hurt, digging into him like a burn that went so deep into his nerve endings that all he ended up feeling was numb, which was better than the pain. Diyomendon's harsh grip around his wrist was grounding, and so Rezekyrios followed his eldest brother and felt his heartbeat and breathing calm as the numbness overwhelmed everything else.

YTHIRIS, AS A MOTHER, couldn't help but worry about her children. Especially as the number of Accursed attacks continued increasing and the fear that there would be another Great Calamity became ever larger.

Her children were so young, her eldest barely seventeen and her youngest not quite eight. A part of her wished she could protect them from the entire world.

But they were the children of a king, born into great responsibility, and she knew that she couldn't shield them. It would be vain to try, and would only have made it even more difficult for them.

They were her and Agamenjiyr's children, and they would be fine. Their father had become king when he was barely older than Tmra was now. Her husband was the strongest man she'd ever known, and their children were strong, too.

She did worry. She was a mother; she couldn't help it. She loved and cared for them so much her entire heart ached and overflowed with it.

She worried that Tdroki's anger would consume him. She worried that Rkalla would maneuver her way into trouble that she wouldn't be able to get out from. She worried that Nkidu would be killed. She worried that Tmra wouldn't find his way.

She couldn't help but worry, but she knew also that they were strong, and when she saw them with each other, helping and supporting one another, she couldn't help but feel that there was absolutely nothing they wouldn't be able to overcome.

AGAMENJIYR HAD WISHED his children an easier life than his own. It looked like that wouldn't be happening. With the way the Accursed attacks were increasing, it was likely that their lives would be at least as difficult. Potentially even more so.

It made him wonder why he'd even wished an easier life for them. None of his satisfaction with his life had ever come from things being easy. All of his pride, all of his fulfillment, came from the difficult challenges he had overcome. From the things he had achieved despite incredible adversity.

He no longer wished his children an easy life. He hoped instead that they would live fulfilling lives in which every hardship they faced made them stronger.

DIYOMENDON CAME ACROSS Luxanthus and Rezekyrios in the hall. Luxanthus was kneeling down in front of Rezekyrios and had his hands on the younger boy's arms. He looked at a complete loss of what to do, which wasn't a good look on him, Daimmu-Blessed as he was.

Rezekyrios, who was the source of the problem at hand, as he always seemed to be, was tense and shaking. His two different-colored eyes were flicking around, and the kohl around them was smudged, which meant he'd been rubbing at them again.

"I just want to be able to help," the young boy said, his voice cracking as he shook harder. It was obvious that Luxanthus had absolutely no idea what to do. But of course he wouldn't. The Daimmu-Blessed had never in his life known what it felt like to not be able to do anything.

With the kingdom being attacked by increasing numbers of Accursed with increasing frequency, Luxanthus was still able to do something about it. Unlike the rest of them, who were feeling increasingly helpless.

Rezekyrios looked like he was about to crumble apart from the anxiety of that, and Diyomendon hissed out a breath. "You're not the only one who feels like that, Rezekyrios," he said sharply, because when the young boy got like that, nothing but a loud, forceful tone was able to penetrate whatever was going on in his head.

"Everyone is feeling like that," Diyomendon told him firmly, putting a hand on his youngest brother's shoulder. He looked down at Luxanthus, who was blinking up at him, looking lost but also relieved at his presence. Also not good expressions on him.

"Except for Luxanthus there," Diyomendon said forcefully, narrowing his eyes at the young warrior, whose own eyes widened in response. "He feels fine." He narrowed his eyes further, and Luxanthus's expression closed off, becoming perfectly, utterly blank.

Satisfied that the Daimmu-Blessed had gotten his message, Diyomendon turned his gaze back to Rezekyrios.

"The rest of us feel awful, though," he said, still harshly. The young boy needed to get it through his head that it wasn't just he who was feeling helpless. Diyomendon took the boy's wrist and tugged him sharply, as Rezekyrios was looking all over the place like the torches on the walls had been blown out and he was submerged in complete darkness and unable to see anything. "Come on," Diyomendon said, pulling him, "Luxanthus has work to do. Let's not hold him back with our uselessness."

It took several moments of basically dragging the young boy along until Rezekyrios finally stopped stumbling and managed to get his feet under him, falling into step beside Diyomendon. When Diyomendon looked down at him, the young boy's black and yellow-orange eyes were still sightless, but they'd stopped flicking wildly, now settled on the ground in front of his feet, which Diyomendon figured was some amount of improvement.

Diyomendon took his brother back to the royal study where he'd been working. He'd grown frustrated and fed up with his work, so he'd been heading out to take a walk in the palace gardens to stretch his legs and clear his head. Then he'd run into Luxanthus and Rezekyrios in the hall. Subsequent change of plans.

So now he was back in the study. He sat Rezekyrios down at the table where he'd been sitting, set a blank scroll in front of him, and pushed the inkwell and reed pen closer to him.

Rezekyrios stared at the items blankly.

"Look, I know you have trouble reading, but you can write, can't you?" Diyomendon said, brushing a hand back through his hair in irritation. "My hand is tired. Be my scribe."

Rezekyrios blinked, raising his two different-colored eyes to look at him, fixing on his face and finally seeming actually to see him.

When the young boy's eyes focused like that, his stare was unnervingly intense. Probably had something to do with the contrast between the dark black eye and the light yellow-orange one, and the way he hardly seemed to blink. It made Diyomendon feel like the boy was looking straight into his soul.

Diyomendon sighed, lowering his arm. "Look, all you have to do is write exactly what I say, okay?"

The boy just needed something to do. Some way to feel useful so his feelings of guilt and helplessness didn't obliterate him.

Diyomendon knew firsthand how terrible those feelings were. And Rezekyrios had it even worse than he did.

Also, his hand really was tired from writing.

The young boy's brow furrowed slightly, and he started chewing on his lower lip. "My handwriting is bad," he mumbled, lowering his intense gaze.

Diyomendon exhaled derisively. "Do I look like I care if the advisers have trouble reading it?" he asked, and Rezekyrios blinked and then looked back up at him, different-colored eyes flicking over his face.

Diyomendon gave him a malicious, conspiratorial grin. "Make it as messy as you want," he said, and he laughed slightly, feeling suddenly delightedly vengeful and maybe even giddy. "It would serve them right." He met his little brother's intent gaze. "My ideas are better than their shitty ones anyway, no matter how nicely they write theirs out. Their proposals could be in the most elegantly written handwriting in existence, and it still wouldn't make their shit ideas any better."

He looked away and snorted, sneering as he let himself feel furious at people's incompetence for a moment. When he looked back at his little brother, the boy still looked uncertain, though, still worried at his lip hard enough that the flesh caught between his teeth was white.

Diyomendon decided to take a different tactic, shrugging and shaking his writing hand pointedly, wrist and fingers limp. "Honestly, though, Rezekyrios, with my hand as tired as it is, your handwriting is probably better than mine at this point."

The boy was looking at him in utter perplexity. "You could get a scribe," he pointed out.

"The scribes can go die," Diyomendon snapped, anger flaring at the very idea of having to deal with any of them or see their stupid, vapid faces.

Rezekyrios still looked doubtful and anxious, and Diyomendon started to feel frustrated. He hissed, glaring at his younger brother. "And what are you complaining for, anyway?" he said tetchily. "You said you wanted to be helpful, didn't you?" Rezekyrios's eyes widened slightly, and Diyomendon gestured to the ink and papyrus. "So make yourself useful and help me out by writing what I tell you."

That finally seemed to get through to the boy; Rezekyrios let go of chewing on his lip and reached for the reed pen sticking up out of the ink well.

Diyomendon exhaled, tension that he hadn't realized was there leaving his shoulders.

For the next few hours, Diyomendon dictated reports and proposals to his little brother, who wrote down everything dutifully. When the young boy's hand started shaking and Diyomendon suggested they take a break, Rezekyrios resolutely shook his head and simply switched hands, starting to write with his left instead of his right. It had stunned Diyomendon, before he remembered that when Rezekyrios was first starting to learn to write, he'd written with his left hand, before switching to using the right because that was the hand that everyone else used.

Well, if his little brother was that desperate to carry out a productive task, Diyomendon certainly wasn't going to deny him, so he continued dictating to the younger boy.

They only finally stopped once it had grown dark. Rezekyrios's head was nodding and he kept rubbing at his eyes with his wrists to try to keep himself awake. It made an absolute mess of the kohl.

Diyomendon sighed, pulling the reed pen from his little brother's hand. "All right, that's enough," he said firmly. Rezekyrios looked absolutely distraught and opened his mouth to object, but Diyomendon shook his head. "My brain is burnt to a blackened crisp; I can't possibly think anymore," he said, and Rezekyrios closed his mouth.

Diyomendon sighed again, reaching out and ruffling the boy's hair, flicking one of the braided strands weighted down with a gold bead. "You're better than this, you know," he told the boy, voice softer. "You're not an idiot, Rezekyrios."

The boy blinked his different-colored eyes, looking at him intently, and Diyomendon prodded him lightly in the forehead. "People are going to tell you that you shouldn't think about things so much," he continued, looking at his little brother meaningfully, "but I am going to tell you that you should use that head of yours more."

Rezekyrios's brow furrowed and his lip caught between his teeth again. Diyomendon shifted his gaze away, letting the boy absorb his words.

It wasn't Rezekyrios's fault that there wasn't any role for him in the palace. Unfortunately, the world wasn't fair, and nobody was going to be able to carve a place that fit him. Everyone else undervalued him anyway, seeing only his clumsiness and his difficulty focusing, and missing the way he saw things that other people didn't and thought about things in ways that nobody else did.

If Rezekyrios wanted a place in the world, he'd have to figure it out for himself. Nobody else would be able to do it for him.

The boy's mind was his greatest asset. All he had to do was use it.

Diyomendon absently picked up one of the scrolls that his little brother had filled, looking it over. He laughed slightly when he saw the handwriting. "By the Daimmu, Rezekyrios—your handwriting isn't even as bad as some of the shit I've seen on the reports those idiots give me." He glanced back at the boy, who was rubbing his eyes. As if the black smeared in his eye-sockets and over the backs of his wrists wasn't already bad enough by that point. It was absolutely unbecoming of a Prince and anyone who saw it would probably have a heart attack.

Sighing, Diyomendon walked over and pushed his younger brother out of the chair. "Go wash your face and then get in bed before you pass out and hit your head on something," he said, and Rezekyrios nodded obediently and left.

Diyomendon watched him go and then took a moment to close his eyes, exhaling out his nose. His mind felt like it was filled with heavy smoke.

He opened his eyes again and rolled back his shoulders. He should take his own advice and get some sleep. It wouldn't do to pass out and hit the head of the sacred crown prince and future king on something.

Actually, maybe he should let himself pass out.

THE SUN HAD PASSED the midpoint in the sky before Naliki was able to find her youngest brother.

When she finally found him, it was in the shadow of one of the palace's outer pillars, in a location that allowed a distant view of the training arena.

"Hey, Tmra," she said, making him startle slightly as he turned to look at her with wide eyes.

She'd always found the dark one fascinating. It was such a solid black, like the eye of a cobra, and she couldn't read it or tell where it was looking.

Since she was always trying to read him, though, she usually looked at the lighter yellow-orange eye.

"I brought you something," she said, holding out a honey-and-date cake that she had wrapped in a cloth.

He took the parcel, glancing at it in his hands before looking back up at her. "How did you find me?" he asked. He was doing that thing where he worried at his lower lip with his teeth.

She reached out and lightly brushed her thumb over his lip so he'd realize what he was doing and stop chewing on it. "You think I haven't also figured out all the best places from which to watch the training arena unobserved?" she lied with a smile.

She hadn't before, but she'd probably discovered them all now. She'd spent so long that day looking for Tmra.

Now that Tmra's lip was no longer caught between his teeth, he looked at her with his mouth parted slightly, black eye unreadable and yellow-orange eye mistrustful. He returned his attention to the parcel in his hands and carefully untied it to reveal the small honey cake with its top layer of date pieces.

"I figured you'd be watching him," Naliki said, nodding to the training arena where Nkidu had been spending all day every day for the past several months. Taking a moment to pay attention to the action down below, she saw that the fifteen-year-old was busy fighting an entire unit of adult warriors by himself. She whistled low, raising her eyebrows slightly. "Our middle brother's really amazing, huh?"

Tmra didn't answer; he was staring down at the cake in his hands. The readable parts of his expression were doubtful and wary.

Naliki rolled her eyes, feeling stung at his blatant distrust. "It's not poisoned," she informed him, possibly a bit pettishly.

"I don't think you'd poison it," Tmra said, shaking his head, though he was still looking at the cake dubiously. "I just. Was wondering why you brought it for me." He glanced up at her. "Thank you, though," he said, somehow managing to make that phrase utterly despondent. It was crushing.

Even worse was the way he then took a bite of the cake like he was forcing himself to, swallowed without hardly chewing and probably without having tasted it, and then looked her in the eye and stated, "It's good."

Naliki snorted, affronted. "Of course it's good; it's honey cake with dates."

Tmra looked down and took another obliging bite. He once again chewed and swallowed like he wasn't tasting it.

Naliki exhaled, feeling disappointed, bitter, and also resentful. She knew that he didn't feel comfortable around her and didn't seem to like her much, but she'd brought him the cake to try to be nice.

"Look, answer me honestly, okay?" she said, looking at him without much hope. "Do I scare you, Tmra?"

He glanced up at her briefly, then looked back down at the cake, though now he didn't even seem to be seeing it. "You don't scare me," he seemed to decide on, brow furrowing slightly. "You're just confusing."

His teeth caught on his lower lip again, and Naliki sighed, brushing her thumb over the chapped skin as a gentle reminder for him to stop. "So are you," she told him tiredly.

She really didn't know how to deal with him, and it killed her.

Case in point: at her statement, he suddenly blinked in a moment of some kind of realization, different-colored eyes widening slightly, and said, "Oh."

Naliki felt a little stunned, a little puzzled, and a little curious. "'Oh'?"

He met her gaze, and then looked away again. "I'm sorry," he said, with a balmy weight that was strikingly different from the usual automatic, panic-stricken apologies he was prone to blurting. "I didn't realize."

Naliki didn't get what he meant, but she just sighed. "If you're sorry about that, then I'm sorry, too," she said. She gestured at the cake and offered a small, possibly slightly ironic smile. "Consider the cake an apology and a peace offering."

"Okay," agreed Tmra with surprising ease. He looked up at her earnestly and said, "Then let's share it."

Naliki blinked at him, then her expression softened. "Okay," she accepted, and Tmra's responding smile made her heart feel warm, sticky, and sweet, like the half of the honey cake that he broke off and shared with her.

They ate their portions of the baked treat while watching their middle brother drop fully grown and fully trained warriors into the dirt.

They finished and licked the honey from their fingers. Naliki tried to think of something else to say, but couldn't.

The sun was lowering in the sky. "I...guess I should get going," she said awkwardly. It didn't quite seem like the right thing to say, but she couldn't stay, and she couldn't leave without saying anything.

"Okay," said Tmra easily, keeping his gaze on Nkidu and not looking at her. "Thank you again for the cake."

"Of course!" Naliki said with a brightness she didn't feel. She turned to leave.

As she did, she glanced back over her shoulder at him. He was still standing there in the shade of the column, watching the action in the training arena below with a kind of profound stillness.

Viewing him in profile like that, she could see only his solid-black eye—the one that looked like it belonged to a cobra.

She'd never felt scared of him before, but she walked away from him that day fighting off unexplainable shivers.

TMRA MUST HAVE seen or heard the branches of the fig tree shiver, because as he walked below it he looked up, straight at where

Luxanthus was perched on one of the lower branches with a ripe fig between his teeth.

The younger boy blinked up at him. "Nkidu?"

Luxanthus blinked back down at him. He removed the fig from his mouth and greeted, "Tmra."

The younger boy's messy brown hair had fallen over his right eye, such that only his yellow-orange one was visible. It was the eye that made him look like an owl. Especially when he tilted his head quizzically, as he was doing at that moment. "What are you doing?"

"Picking figs," Luxanthus answered, holding up a cloth satchel full of the fruits. "I'm on a short break from training, so I thought I'd eat something. There are a lot of ripe figs right now." He hopped down out of the tree, landing lightly on the ground. "It wouldn't be good to eat too much before going back to fighting," he admitted, and held the satchel out to his younger brother. "I have extras. You can share them with Diyomendon and Rkalla."

Tmra took the satchel of figs, looking down at them before looking back up at him. His hair drifted out of his right eye slightly so that the dark one became visible as well. He opened his mouth and started, "I..." but then trailed off.

Luxanthus looked down at him, feeling a dark hollowness in his chest. The last time they'd talked had been when Tmra had run into him in the hall, and then proceeded to fall apart while Luxanthus could do nothing to stop it. His presence had seemed to make it worse.

He knew that he was the only one who could fight the Accursed. He wished that that would make people feel better, instead of seeming to make them feel worse. He wished they'd feel glad that he was capable of fighting so that they didn't have to, instead of only feeling guilty for not being in his place.

He was supposed to make people feel reassured and safe. Instead, he made everyone feel horrible. He hated it.

He looked away from his younger brother. He wanted to say

something. Only, reassurances didn't seem to help. He wondered if there was anything he could say.

He missed hanging out with his younger brother. He didn't have the time, anymore. It was necessary, but it hurt.

He wanted to say something. He thought about what thoughts he used to reassure himself when he started to feel distraught, and started, "Once I defeat the Accursed and Ordyuk is safe again..." He met his younger brother's owlish gaze, Tmra's bangs having fallen back over his dark eye from the curious angle of his head. "Let's go boating on the Aru River," Luxanthus said.

He'd always used to love doing that. He remembered Tmra enjoying it, too.

Looking up at him, the younger boy said, "Okay."

Luxanthus looked back at him, feeling keenly how much he'd missed him, and looked away. "I'm sorry," he said, because there was nothing more he could do.

Tmra smiled at him in a way that indicated he understood. "Me, too."

Luxanthus looked at that yellow-orange gaze, and then away again. He found himself looking up at the branches of the fig tree above him. They were too thin and far out from the trunk for him to have reached them climbing the tree, and, since he knew his physical abilities very well, he could tell that they were slightly too high for him to reach them by jumping. He glanced back at his younger brother, and nodded up at the ripe figs slightly too far above him. "Think we can reach those figs, if you sit on my shoulders and I jump?" he asked.

Tmra looked up at the figs above them, looked back at Luxanthus, and smiled. "Yeah."

Luxanthus's own lips curved in return, and he got down onto one knee and leaned forward slightly, Tmra putting his hands on his shoulders and then hopping up onto them, Luxanthus resting his hands firmly slightly above his younger brother's knees and then standing. He looked up at the figs above them, bent his legs, and jumped.

Tmra reached up above him, grabbing on to a clump of the fruits. Gravity pulled them back down, but Tmra held on, and the figs came down with him.

Luxanthus landed lightly on his feet and then crouched down, and his younger brother slipped down from his shoulders, bunches of the ripe fruits in both hands. Luxanthus turned to look at him and smiled. Tmra mirrored him.

"Good work," Luxanthus said, ruffling his little brother's hair. He said honestly, "I couldn't have reached those without you."

Tmra's eyes softened, understanding. "Same to you." He set the figs down atop the satchel.

He straightened, and Luxanthus, still crouched, found himself leaning his head against his younger brother's back, between his shoulder blades. The gold and gems of the boy's elaborate beaded collar-piece pressed uncomfortably against his forehead, but he didn't care. "Thank you, Tmra," he voiced softly.

Sometimes he felt so tired.

Then he thought of Tmra, and he felt like he could strike down the very sun.

He felt the flex of his younger brother's ribs as Tmra exhaled. "It's okay." Tmra stepped forward and then turned, stepping back in and wrapping his arms around Luxanthus's neck, the gold bangles around his wrists and arms cold against Luxanthus's heated skin. "It's okay," the younger boy repeated, and leaned his cheek down against the top of Luxanthus's head. "I can be strong, too."

Luxanthus exhaled, his forehead against his younger brother's collarbones, inhaling the scents of perfume and gold. "I know it," he said, absolutely certain of it. He gave himself a moment to breathe and hold his eyes closed, and then pulled away and stood, opening his eyes to look down at his younger brother and appear as assured as he was able. "Let's reach even greater heights one day, Tmra," he said.

Tmra looked up at him and smiled. "Yeah."

His hair was fallen over his dark eye, and Luxanthus brushed it back behind Tmra's ear so that he could see that eye, too. Both the owlish yellow-orange one as well as the deep-black one.

Luxanthus gave him one last quirk of his lips and then turned to head back to the training arena.

The sooner he defeated the Accursed, the sooner he and his little brother could again go boating together.

The only problem was that the Accursed attacks would have to get even worse before he was allowed to fight them.

Luxanthus didn't hate much about the world, but he did hate that he had to wish for the situation to get worse just to be able to spend time with his brother again.

IV

REZEKYRIOS WAS AWARE of the fact that he saw the world differently from other people.

There was maybe more than one example of this, but one of the ones he was aware of was that other people seemed to be able to make out a lot more in the darkness than he could.

He'd always had trouble seeing anything in the dark. It was like every line and edge disintegrated and blew into the air like dust that darted around in front of his eyes from his breaths, making it so he couldn't see the contours of objects. If he tried to focus on anything, the bright specks collected and gathered there, pulsing in thousands upon thousands of tiny coruscations along with the beating of his heart.

Perhaps it should have scared him, since he couldn't see anything around him or where he was going, but it didn't. If anything, it made him feel calm, sometimes even comforted, and he could navigate well enough using the information he got from the feel of the ground beneath his feet, from the sounds around him, from the feel of the air against his skin.

The world was more bearable when its hard lines and blinding light were reduced to darkness and breath-swirled dust. Less painful. Rezekyrios had always used to like the night, because of that.

The night was no longer so calming now that it was filled with yells and screams; now that when he looked outside at the city, it was stabbingly bright from the fire of so many torches. In those puddles of painful light Rezekyrios could sometimes see the monstrous forms of the Accursed skitter and crawl. Hard lines and blinding light, and Rezekyrios wished it would go back to being soft darkness and harmless dust.

THE SITUATION WITH THE ACCURSED was getting worse.

They were attacking in small hordes most nights, now, with enough regularity that the nights when they didn't were almost worse than those they did. And the monsters were starting to show up deeper and deeper within the city, rather than only attacking from the desert edge.

Fear, panic, and sorrow were growing even more quickly than the body count. More terrible than those who were simply killed were those who were attacked but survived, who then had to either kill themselves or have someone kill them before they turned into Accursed. Worse still was when they weren't killed fast enough and did become monsters, turning on their own acquaintances and family members.

The people of Ordyuk were praying to the Daimmu, but it was clear that the Daimmu were dealing with strife amongst themselves as well. The elements were acting up and warring against one another: the river with the earth, the wind with the clouds and desert dunes, the rain with the fire, the animals with the insects and arachnids. Only those Daimmu who ruled such human matters as the arts, architecture, music, and dance could be called upon for direct assistance, and all they could provide was inspiration and what amount of hope and comfort those mental recourses provided.

In such times of crisis and disaster, the arts always flourished. They were all that people had.

It reminded Ythiris of her nightmares: the dreams from which she'd always awoken with her face awash in tears.

She herself never died in these dreams. She only ever danced over corpses and ruins as the world came to an end around her. In these nightmares, she could never do anything but dance—over the ashes of Ordyuk, over the lifeless bodies of her people, her husband, her children. Their lifeless eyes stared up at her sightlessly and she danced over empty stares and stepped more cracks into their shattered bones, feeling their bodies crunch and bleed beneath her toes.

Every day in Ordyuk there were funeral pyres. The scent of burning bodies permeated the city. The charred remains were dumped into mass graves that were left open because there was no point in burying them when the next day there would only be more.

Many people in the streets trembled, threw themselves to the ground, and cried. Others stood tall, supported each other, laughed and sang and danced, defiant and determined.

It reminded Ythiris of falling in love: of watching the young Agamenjiyr, newly appointed king, walk barefoot with squared shoulders and raised chin down the blood-soaked main street of the city, his hands held slightly out to his sides, loose-fingered and open for all those who wished to reach out and brush their hands over his, take comfort in the fact that he was there—corporeal, assured, and determined.

"The Great Calamity is over," he'd told them, "and we here have survived. We are alive, and as long as we are alive, so is Ordyuk. This is not the end. This is a beginning. Beginnings are always more difficult than endings. Prepare yourselves for the difficulties that we will have to overcome, because there will be difficulties—and we will overcome them."

Ythiris remembered those gold-orange eyes of his falling on her like the light of candles after what had been complete darkness; she remembered the way they had given her the strength to lift herself from the bloodstained dirt and dance.

Agamenjiyr had been, for all these years, her life-giving warmth and light. She'd taken that flame into herself, felt it grow, had given it new life and form in the bodies and souls of their children: those four wondrous entities who were as strong and beautiful as the blazes from which they'd been born.

The attacks from the Accursed were getting worse, but in the darkness of every night, Agamenjiyr was warmth and light against her skin—corporeal, assured, and determined.

She traced her fingers over his face, laid her head down on his chest, and felt his heart beating: a rhythm more infallible than the ceaseless flickering of living flame.

"The kingdom will survive. And our children."

"I know."

THE SITUATION WITH THE ACCURSED was getting worse.

Agamenjiyr was tired. He kept walking.

He couldn't remember ever not feeling tired. He couldn't remember ever wanting to sleep. He couldn't remember ever finding any comfort in the empty darkness behind his eyes. He couldn't remember ever opening his eyes without his eyelids feeling heavy. He couldn't remember ever opening his eyes to the sun rising over his desert kingdom of Ordyuk and not finding it beautiful.

He couldn't remember ever looking at the people under his rule and not feeling the weight of all those lives and the burden of responsibility for all those fates. He couldn't remember ever looking at his people and not feeling the power and energy of those lives and his delight at being responsible for all their legacies.

He couldn't remember the horror of the Great Calamity ever not being a constant presence lingering like a waking nightmare in the back of his mind. He couldn't remember ever not being driven forward by it, chasing the light so that the shadows would fall behind him and never ahead.

He couldn't remember ever not feeling like he might push himself till he dropped. He couldn't remember any of that strain or pain ever forcing him to stop.

The situation with the Accursed was getting worse. Agamenjiyr was tired.

He was reminded of spiders, and the effort they put into creating intricate, elaborate webs that were then blown away in the wind.

He was reminded of birds, and the way they looked like pathetic, small, ugly things as they molted, before new feathers grew in and made them appear once again magnificent, large, and resplendent.

He was reminded of stunning and mighty temples that crumbled apart to ruin, of great and mighty beasts that decayed away to skeletons, buried by the desert's shifting sands.

He was reminded of snakes, the way they became pale and started to crack and crumble apart like sandstone before it was revealed to be nothing but old skin, peeling away to reveal a new, brighter, and larger being beneath.

He was reminded of clouds that formed noble phantasms or terrible storms in the sky, and then were blown away to reveal the sun shining behind.

The situation with the Accursed was getting worse. Agamenjiyr was tired.

He remembered walking streets filled with corpses and throwing up stomach acid in front of his subjects. He remembered mustering up his dignity as he straightened, wiping his mouth and saying, "Okay, that was my low point; the good news is that things can't get any worse than that: which means that they will only get better from here on out." He remembered laughter that was not unkind, and someone handing him a bottle of beer with which to wash out his mouth.

He remembered seeing those same streets that had made him vomit make a young girl dance. He remembered falling in love with those bloody toes, those crying burgundy eyes, and that life-awed smile. He remembered when fingers had slipped teasingly between his own and pulled him after them. Ythiris, the dawn to his every night.

He couldn't remember ever waking up not feeling tired—but he couldn't remember ever waking up and wishing he hadn't opened his eyes.

He remembered the first time he'd seen his first son open his, an infant with red-orange eyes who, already bitterly disappointed with life's inadequacies, started to cry immediately.

Diyomendon had spent the first few years of his life crying. He'd spent the rest alternating between furious yelling, livid hisses, and enraged silences.

Naliki had spent most of her childhood laughing at him.

It was rare that any of them had seen Luxanthus laugh, and none of them had ever seen him cry; not at any point in his life. Even as an infant, he'd been preternaturally calm and quiet.

Rezekyrios was the only one who had screamed.

Now they were older, but Diyomendon still raged, Naliki still laughed, and Luxanthus was still calm and quiet. Rezekyrios had years ago stopped screaming.

The situation with the Accursed was getting worse. Agamenjiyr was tired.

He kept walking.

"The kingdom will survive," Ythiris said, looking at him. "And our children."

"I know."

And so he kept on walking.

"The situation is going to keep getting worse," Diyomendon said, looking at him. "It's not going to stop."

"I know."

And so he kept on walking.

"So, the world really sucks right now," Naliki said, looking at him. "But the music is really great."

"I know."

And so he kept on walking.

"I'm not scared," Rezekyrios said, looking at him. "I'm frustrated."

"I know."

And so he kept on walking.

"You need to let me go out there," Luxanthus said, looking at him. "You can't afford not to anymore."

"I know."

And so he kept on walking.

"You're the king," those eyes told him.

He knew.

That was why he kept on walking.

WHEN NOBODY WAS LOOKING, Diyomendon pushed the rest of his food onto Luxanthus's plate.

"I'm not hungry," he mumbled, when the Daimmu-Blessed warrior looked at him quizzically. "Also, you need it more than me."

Luxanthus was out every night fighting the Accursed, now.

During those hours, Diyomendon was sleeping. Or at least trying to. Pretending to. Mostly he lay there feeling like he was burning up from the inside with all his fury.

He got up from the table. "I'm done eating," he said, and left the hall.

He went back up to his chambers and locked the door.

Naliki forced her way in, as she always did. Locked doors couldn't stop her from entering.

At least she always locked them again after her, though.

"You know, if you keep all that hate and anger inside, it's going to eat you alive, Tdroki," she said, smiling at him in that way she always did, like she wanted to eat him.

It didn't faze him. It never did. It never had.

"Oh? Any bright ideas for what I should do with it, Naliki?" he sneered, glaring at her in the way he always did, like he wished she'd go crawl in a hole and die.

It didn't faze her. It never did. It never had.

She was a cat playing with her food as she said, "As you would tell me: figure it out for yourself."

Diyomendon grinned, all sharpness and malevolence. "That's some good advice. I'd give you some more, except that I know you wouldn't follow it."

Naliki grinned right back, utterly sanguine. "If it's telling me to leave you alone, then it's bad advice; so yeah, I wouldn't follow it."

She never left him alone. Probably nothing in the world could get her to do so.

Not even the Accursed. She was that cursed persistent.

Diyomendon rolled his eyes. "Relax," he said. "I might be no Luxanthus, but I'm not so weak that..." He realized too late that he didn't have an ending to that statement.

Naliki grinned at him like a feline that had a rat caught squirming uselessly beneath its paw. "Not so weak that...?" she purred, sweet as honey and false as a mirage.

His anger flared in flames behind his eyes. "Not so weak that I need you worrying about me," he sneered, lips pulling away from his clenched teeth.

He couldn't claim that he wasn't so weak he would break, when she'd simply call him out on it, knowing as well as he did how close he was to snapping. Burning wood made weak by the fire that was consuming it.

Naliki curled her lips away from her teeth in that hungry way she always did. "I'm not worried," she said, ever so honeyed. "You'd look good burning alive with flame." Her eyes brightened, her voice saccharine. "You do look good burning alive with flame."

Diyomendon hissed a breath through his teeth. "What, by the Daimmu, is that supposed to mean?" His chest was so full of suffocating heat, making it ever so hard to breathe.

"It means that even if you let your hatred and anger eat you alive, I still wouldn't be worried about you."

Diyomendon looked at her. He wanted to throw himself down on the bed and pull a pillow over his face.

Naliki was the only one there, and she didn't care.

Diyomendon threw himself down on the bed and pulled a pillow over his face. "If you're not worried about me, then why do you always follow me?" he asked, muffled.

"Because the fire is so warm!" He felt Naliki hop onto the bed next to him and snuggle against his side. Her fingers traced over the skin of his chest, between the gold and carnelian beading of his elaborate collar-piece. "I like being around you when you're angry."

Diyomendon puffed a breath against the pillow. "So you've said," he mumbled. The air from his exhales was warm and humid trapped against his skin. His every exhale made each inhale progressively more difficult. By the time he mumbled out, "I don't know what to do," he was starting to feel dizzy.

"Aside from give Luxanthus your food?" his sister quipped, and Diyomendon removed the pillow from his face to smack her in the head with it.

"I wasn't hungry," he grumbled. "Luxanthus has never had any problem making up for my inadequacies—so he can make up for my not wanting to eat the food, too. It's not like he'll have any trouble eating it; and he could eat even more, besides."

She lifted her head from his chest to look at him. "You're awfully bitter when it comes to him," she remarked, and Diyomendon shoved the pillow against her face.

"And why shouldn't I be?!" he retorted.

Naliki pushed the pillow aside, laying her body atop it so he couldn't hit her with it again and catching his gaze. "You care about him, though," she pointed out, and Diyomendon seethed.

"And why shouldn't I?!" he demanded, shoving at her. "By the Daimmu, don't try to tell me what I should or shouldn't feel!"

She grabbed his hand and pulled it to her face, closing her teeth lightly over a couple of his fingers and licking them, making Diyomendon hiss again and yank his hand away.

"I'm not," she told him, raising herself up to look down at him, and she wasn't smiling, her expression serious for once.

"Then stop insinuating that you are!" he snapped, and she only broke out into a grin again.

"But it's making you so angry!" she teased, poking his nose. He grabbed her hand and clenched it hard. She didn't so much as flinch, simply looking down at him.

"What do you expect me to do, Naliki?" he said, dark and low. "When you rile me up like this." He held her gaze, his teeth gritted and his words spitting, flaming heat waves simmering in his chest. "What, by the Daimmu, are you trying to get me to do?"

She leaned her cheek against his hand that was clenched over her own. "I'm not trying to make you do anything," she said, holding both his hand and his gaze without flinching. "I just don't want to see what happens if you were to stop being angry."

Her gaze and tone were too serious, and Diyomendon turned his head away, letting his hand go lax around hers. Now she was the one holding his hand there instead of the other way around. His arm would have fallen limp and lifeless against the bed, except that she didn't let it.

"It's not like I'm nothing except for anger, you know," he muttered.

Sometimes he wished he were; it would've been easier.

"I know," she said. She unfolded his unresistant fingers and pressed his limp hand against her cheek, the corner of her jaw settled in the heel of his palm. "But your anger is where you get your power, see?" Her jaw moved against his hand as she spoke. "Your anger is what makes you my favorite brother, and it's your anger that's going to make you a great king."

She moved her head away from his hand, interlacing her fingers with his instead and pushing his arm down against the bed, leaning close to murmur warmly into his ear: "Don't let anyone tell you that you shouldn't feel angry."

She pressed her lips against his brow, and Diyomendon closed his eyes. Her bead-covered breasts were pressed against his chest, her legs intertwined with his, and with the way he felt like he was burning alive she should have felt cold against him, but she felt warm.

He exhaled against the sheets on the bed. "I don't want to be king," he said, tired. He was so sick of everything. The entire world could go down in flames; it would be better off that way.

"Well, there might not be any kingdom for you to become king of, anyway," Naliki said, and she probably didn't know any more than he did to what extent she was being serious and to what extent she was simply mocking him.

"It's not fair," he said.

Naliki, having laid her head down against his shoulder, huffed a breath against his skin. "Which part?" she asked wryly.

Her fingers remained interlaced with his, and he brushed his thumb softly, rhythmically over the back of her hand. "If Ordyuk was going to be destroyed," he said bitterly, "I wanted to do it myself."

It wasn't fair.

NALIKI PRESSED HER LIPS against Tdroki's that night.

It wasn't as if they could sleep when the night was full of shouts and screams, and the kingdom might fall and they might die. The kiss didn't mean anything. She was scared, and she wanted to kiss someone, and she loved Tdroki more than anyone. So she kissed him.

He'd frozen and she'd pulled back, looking down at him. He'd looked up at her in the dark, blinked, and licked his lips.

"What was that for?" he asked.

"Because I wanted to," she said. "And there was no reason not to."

The second time she kissed him, he kissed her gently back. It made her smile. It was the first time she'd done so genuinely in months, and it made Tdroki huff, and she could count on one hand how many times she could remember him even doing that much.

Like they'd used to when they were kids, they fell asleep in each other's arms. When she awakened first, she bit her brother's shoulder. His eyes flew open as he bolted upright with a shout and pushed her bodily off the bed, proceeding to curse at her while she curled up on the ground laughing so hard that tears streamed from her eyes.

The Accursed attacks may have been getting progressively worse, and it was obvious that they would only continue to do so, but she hadn't felt that truly happy in a long time.

LUXANTHUS, WHEN KILLING the Accursed, felt like himself in a way he never felt when doing anything else. The world made sense and everything within it felt perfectly aligned. He couldn't imagine himself doing anything else. He couldn't imagine himself wanting to do anything else.

The Accursed fell to his blades like notes and chords being played from the instruments of musicians.

Everyone around him was growing ever more frustrated, ever more afraid, and ever more exhausted, beginning to unravel and fall to pieces. Luxanthus, however, felt himself growing ever more pleased, ever more confident, and ever more energized, like the disconnected pieces of him were finally coming together.

The situation with the Accursed was growing worse with every passing day, and Luxanthus was the only person who honestly didn't mind.

If there was a reason that he'd been brought into the world, it had been entirely for this.

THE SITUATION WITH THE ACCURSED was growing worse with every passing day, and Rezekyrios didn't feel quite sane. Something in him was crumbling.

He couldn't remember the last time he'd slept. The nights were too full of fire and shouts and screams and the singing of insects. The skin beneath Rezekyrios's eyes was dark with more than kohl— although there was plenty of kohl there, too. His eyes had been aching like crazy, and he couldn't stop rubbing them and smearing the black everywhere. They didn't even tell him not to anymore. They'd given up on it, and there were more important things to worry about than how much he failed even the simplest duties of a prince. That was okay with him, because he didn't care about that, either. He'd used to. Used to.

Nothing seemed to matter, anymore. Rezekyrios felt distanced from himself. From his body, from his emotions, from his thoughts. The world was surreal. People were crumbling. Diyomendon was quiet hot coals spread darkly over the ground, everywhere. Naliki's every word was like honey and salt rubbed into a wound. Nkidu came back every morning with blood on his skin that wasn't his and humming on his breath some new tune he'd heard. King Agamenjiyr never stopped moving. High Priestess Ythiris still visited temples and prayed to the Daimmu, even though they didn't appear capable of doing very much.

Rezekyrios had taken to going with her, since he didn't have anything else to do. She also was the only one who always welcomed his company—not even Nkidu, who instead spent the nights fighting and the days sleeping.

Rezekyrios and Ythiris were now in the Temple of Silbalmu, the Daimu of Beasts and one of Ordyuk's main protector deities. Silbalmu was the Daimu that people were counting on most, because when Silbalmu was pleased, the dogs, cats, and wild animals would attack the Accursed as well, and were protected by Silbalmu's blessing.

In the Temple of Silbalmu, usually animals were killed, quickly and painlessly, and then offered into the bonfire rising up out of the large depression in the center of the temple's floor, surrounded by giant glass statues of magnificent beasts. The sacrificial animals would be offered along with sacred herbs so that their smoke and essences would permeate the boundary between realms to reach the Daimmu.

That day, Ythiris also cut one of her wrists and let her own blood drip into the fire.

"What are you doing?" Rezekyrios asked her.

She essentially told him that she was offering her blood to the Daimu to show devotion, passion, and conviction. Left unsaid was the part about it showing desperation. Rezekyrios turned his head and looked back into the fire.

If he were a Daimu, he wouldn't be satisfied with a bit of blood. That wouldn't have indicated any kind of conviction to him.

He hadn't been feeling sane, as of late. It felt like something in him had been crumbling away. He felt distanced from his body, his emotions, his thoughts.

He didn't think very much before throwing himself into the fire. All he was thinking was that if a show of desperation and conviction would please the Daimu enough to offer more assistance against the scourge of Accursed, then he would do so, not with some paltry drippings of blood but with a complete self-immolation that the

Daimu could not possibly ignore.

He just wanted to help, really, and he'd been painfully aware for his entire life that he was utterly useless and had absolutely no purpose. If his death, at the very least, could serve some kind of use that would benefit the kingdom he'd grown up in and loved, then he'd offer his life without hesitation.

Ythiris was screaming behind him, but Rezekyrios laughed in pleased and giddy satisfaction as the flames so burningly devoured his flesh, because finally, finally his life had meaning. His laughter was one of pain, but also one of intense relief at having successfully found a way that he could be useful.

He hadn't exactly been feeling sane. But having a reason for his existence was all he'd ever wanted, and so in determining one for himself he was inexorably delighted and completely without regret.

As he burned alive, for the first time in his life Rezekyrios felt significant.

"TMRA!"

Ythiris's heart broke along with her voice as she cried for him, watching him burn alive—the flames licking and biting his skin black while he danced amid the burning acacia and tamarisk, his shrieking laughter tearing apart the very air so that there was hardly any left that could be breathed.

Some of Ythiris's attendants rushed forward, to either pull Tmra from the flames or to quench the fire, but Ythiris raised her hand, stopping them. To abort the sacrifice would be an insult both to Silbalmu and to her son. Tmra had chosen the fate for himself.

Ythiris felt all kinds of pain, in that moment. Her soul was shredded with it. It pained her that her precious Tmra, not even nine years of age, had seen no greater worth in his life than to be a sacrifice; it pained her when she realized that he might even be right; it pained her because it may have been her fault, because she'd been taking him with her to the temples—because she'd seen how desperate he was to do something—and yet she hadn't realized just how desperate he'd been; it pained her to see the body of the beautiful boy she'd borne into the world burn away; it pained her to hear his delighted laughter and realize she couldn't remember the last time she'd heard it; it pained her because she was gladdened to see him dying like this, instead of the way she saw him die in her nightmares, torn apart by the Accursed and screaming from terror.

If her dear, sweet Tmra had to die, she was so painfully glad that it was by his own choice: that it was in laughter and satisfaction rather than in screams and helplessness; that it was for a greater purpose than to become the simple meal of a monster.

Ythiris had never loved her son more than she did while watching him burn. She was filled with so much love and so much pain that she couldn't stand it, and she grabbed one of the bottles of sacrificial wine and downed half of it before throwing the rest over the flame and her burning, laughing, shrieking son. The fire roared higher with the pitch of Tmra's laughing screams.

Ythiris couldn't stand it: all the love and all the pain tearing her apart from the inside. It was so much larger than her body, so much larger than could be contained inside her.

And so she danced, with her unbearable feelings imbuing her limbs, exuding and releasing from her movements. She danced to release everything that couldn't fit inside her mortal body; she danced to become bigger than herself; she danced to the sound of her son's laughing shrieks, hoping that Silbalmu understood how great of a sacrifice Tmra was. Her darling Tmra, who had always been so sensitive, so genuine and observant.

She'd watched him die so many times in her nightmares, and she was crying as she danced, because if he'd seen the same fates for himself that she had seen, she couldn't help but understand why he'd thrown himself into the flames. Why he'd want to die like this, offering himself to the Daimu that was their best bet at assistance against the Accursed, rather than be devoured by the monsters that he didn't have the strength or skill to fight.

Ythiris had borne such an incredible son into the world. It destroyed her to watch him be erased from it. And so she danced, and the flames roared higher with wine, and eventually Tmra's shrieking laughter stopped. Ythiris danced all the harder and the wine-fed flames roared all the higher.

And then there was a fiery flurry, and from the flames flapped a figure that landed lightly on the ground, mottled tawny feathers densely marked with black and creamy-white streaks and blotches along its arms. Mottled light- and dark-brown scales covered areas of its body and blended into bronze skin at the edges. A tuft of feathers poked up on the left side of the figure's head like an ear tuft; dark scales formed a teardrop mark beneath the figure's right eye, which was dark black—the other eye yellow-orange.

Ythiris could barely breathe as she looked at him. "Tmra?" she asked. Her heart was beating so fast, racing.

Her darling Tmra smiled at her like she couldn't remember him ever smiling. "Mother."

She dashed forward and wrapped her arms around him. "By Silbalmu, Tmra..."

He wrapped his arms around her in return, his hands around her back, his nails scratching her slightly, and then—something began to happen. From where her son had scratched her, Ythiris's body began crumbling away.

It was a strange sensation: disintegrating to dust.

Ythiris barely felt anything before she was just...gone.

REZEKYRIOS HAD BEEN burning alive. It had hurt like nothing he'd ever felt, up until it didn't hurt at all.

So you want to be of help, Rezekyrios Tmra Madubabakar?

The voice in his head had been like a hyena's laughter, and

could only have been Silbalmu.

Is there any other reason, Rezekyrios couldn't help but think in return, *that I would have thrown myself into the fire?*

Silbalmu's voice was like a crocodile's rumble: *Are you so eager to die, Tmra?*

If my death is more useful than my life, Rezekyrios thought, *then why shouldn't I?*

Silbalmu's voice like a cheetah's trill: *What if you could help while remaining alive?*

A little late for that, isn't it?

Silbalmu's voice like a jackal's howl: *You're not dead yet, Tmra. I can heal you—no, I can fix you. I can refashion your damaged and disfigured body and give you the power to destroy Jajul's Accursed, and anything else you wish.*

Why? Rezekyrios wondered.

Silbalmu's voice like a cat's purr: *Because you've given yourself over to me completely, and because I can. It's no good, though, unless you actually want it. If you don't, then you won't do anything interesting with it, and there would be no point.*

'Interesting'?

Silbalmu's voice like an asp's hiss: *So tell me, Tmra. Do you want the power to be able to destroy whatever you wish? Would you use it?*

Yes, Rezekyrios thought. *I want it.*

Silbalmu's voice like an eagle owl's hoot: *Good. Then it's yours.*

Rezekyrios felt the pain return all at once, so intense he couldn't even scream. He could feel his body changing; it felt like his flesh was being fiercely yanked and scratched at by sharp claws and teeth.

Silbalmu's voice in his ears like a dog's gleeful yip: *Just remember that in exchange, Tmra, you're* mine.

"Okay," Rezekyrios said. And then: "Oh." His vocal cords were back, it seemed, although his awareness of his body was consumed by pain.

Silbalmu's voice came like an osprey's cry: *Fly, Tmra.*

Rezekyrios flew, and landed lightly on the ground, the flames behind him but a maddening burning and itching caught beneath his skin. He wanted to scratch at it.

His mother was looking at him with shock, disbelief, wonder, hope. "Tmra?" she asked, ever so quiet.

Rezekyrios beamed at her. "Mother." *I'm strong now,* he wanted to say. *I can fight now. I can help.* Somehow, the words didn't make it out; his throat itched and burned. He wanted to scratch at it.

His mother practically leapt on him to pull him into a hug, and Rezekyrios, beaming, hugged her back.

He didn't know if it was because he was itching and burning, or if it was a reflex, but his fingers curled against her back, scratching her with nails that were longer and sharper than he'd realized. And then—his mother crumbled to dust in his arms.

He blinked, surprised and confused, stepping back, looking. There was nothing but a pile of dust on the ground. He looked down at his hands; his nails were like dark talons. His fingers had little feathers on them, mottled brown like the much larger feathers on his arms, the feathers he'd flown with. Areas of his legs and torso were covered in snakelike mottled brown scales.

He looked up at the attendants, priestesses, and priests who were standing there, staring at him with wide, horrified eyes.

"Where's Mother?" Rezekyrios asked them.

One of the women, with a trembling arm, pointed at the pile of dust. Rezekyrios frowned at it. He was still itching and burning maddeningly, and reached up to scratch at his neck; there were scales there. He had to reach higher to the bottom of his jaw to find skin he could scratch.

He looked back at the adults. "What happened?" he asked. He scratched harder; he was really, really itchy. Burningly itchy. It was distracting.

Suddenly one of the men gave a yell and stalked forward, grabbing him roughly and furiously. "You—!"

Rezekyrios gave an alarmed cry and reacted instinctively, scratching at the man to make him let go and back away.

Where his talons scratched the man's arm, the man's body began crumbling away, disintegrating to dust. The decay traveled up the man's arm, overtaking the rest of his body, and in moments he was nothing but a pile of dust on the ground. Rezekyrios stared at it with his mouth fallen open. Then he looked back up at the other adults, and suddenly there was chaos as they scrambled to run, screaming and shouting.

Rezekyrios was burning and itching all over. He reached up, dragging his talons down his scaled neck till he found flesh beneath his collarbone to scratch at, and started to giggle hysterically.

THE MAN WHO BURST into the throne room was panicked, wild-eyed, and distraught. He tried to speak, gesturing wildly, but King Agamenjiyr was only able to catch the names of his wife, youngest son, and the Daimu Silbalmu. It was completely incoherent, but it was enough to ignite a flame of panic in Agamenjiyr's chest. He easily and automatically stomped it down, being much practiced at doing so.

"Calm down," Agamenjiyr told the man, keeping his tone and expression stolid, because as king it was his job to always be the pillar strong enough to hold up a falling sky. "Take six deep breaths. Count them. Then tell me exactly what happened, as succinctly and straightforwardly as possible."

The man looked at Agamenjiyr's stolid expression, found strength there, and did as he was told.

Hearing that his youngest son had thrown himself into the fire and sacrificed himself to Silbalmu only to emerge from the flames covered in scales and feathers and then turned Ythiris and one of the attendants to dust with a touch raised all kinds of feelings in Agamenjiyr, but he stomped them down. He didn't have time for such indulgences. He was the king.

"Go awaken Luxanthus," he said, firm and stolid. "Tell him to forego his morning routine and to meet me outside Silbalmu's Temple with the utmost haste. Inform him only that there's a situation involving Rezekyrios. I will give him the details myself."

The man nodded and ran out of the room. Agamenjiyr stood from his throne, beckoned to his guards, and headed for the temple.

Luxanthus arrived at the location only shortly after they did, having run and leapt across roofs to take the shortest path. He'd clearly come at top speed and was panting slightly when he arrived, but since he was incredibly fit he caught his breath quickly. He'd also done exactly as he'd been told and foregone taking the time to put on his cosmetics and jewelry.

"What's going on?" There was clear panic in Luxanthus's gaze, but he was keeping a hold of himself admirably.

Even standing outside the temple as they were, they could hear the deranged sound of Rezekyrios's laughter echoing from inside.

Luxanthus had always been incredibly controlled and practical, and after Agamenjiyr informed him of the situation, he met Agamenjiyr's gaze resolutely and said, "What do you need me to do?"

"Subdue and restrain him without letting him touch you."

Luxanthus nodded and then turned, taking a step toward the temple, only to pause. Voice lowered, he said, "What's going to happen to him?"

Agamenjiyr was the king. He approached every decision thinking only of what was best for his kingdom. "If his mental state is sound enough and he proves enough coordination to adequately control it, such a power would indubitably be an invaluable weapon against the Accursed," he said. Luxanthus met his gaze, searching, and Agamenjiyr softened his voice. "Be gentle with him, Luxanthus.

He just accidentally killed his own mother; he can't be in the best state of mind. Try not to hold it against him."

Agamenjiyr was emotionally shredded by the loss of his wife. It didn't matter. Rezekyrios hadn't done it by intention, and he could not be held responsible. Agamenjiyr, as king, had long ago steeled himself against all kinds of pain and losses. He had to be always looking forward.

There was understanding in Luxanthus's gaze. "Accidents happen," he acknowledged, quiet and somber as he turned. "At least she wasn't killed by an Accursed."

There was that, too.

Agamenjiyr watched his middle son enter the temple, fingers gripped around the long strip of cloth that he'd been given to bind around his younger brother's fingers. He was not yet sixteen, but he was already a strapping young warrior who could defeat all others in the kingdom. He was also the person with whom Rezekyrios had always been closest. With his physical prowess and his emotional connection to the younger boy, Luxanthus was by far their best bet for subduing a Blessed Rezekyrios.

From the report of Rezekyrios's newly acquired power and the sound of his unhinged laughter, Luxanthus was the only person who could.

Agamenjiyr was tired. The Accursed attacks had been taking a lot out of him. Responding to them as they were happening each night, dealing with the aftermath of them come daylight, trying to prepare for the onslaughts the next night would bring, he couldn't remember the last time he'd slept. He'd only been taking naps here and there, in the occasional less-hectic moment. The loss of Ythiris was a terrible emotional blow; yet the power that Rezekyrios had gained was an undeniable light of hope for the kingdom.

Agamenjiyr watched the temple, waiting for his sons to emerge—ideally both intact.

He was tired and emotionally numb. It didn't matter, though.

Not as long as he could fulfill his duty as king.

His eyelids were heavy and wanted to close, but he kept them open.

LUXANTHUS FOLLOWED the echoing sound of Tmra's wild laughter into Silbalmu's temple, footsteps light and careful. He wasn't sure what to expect, so he tried to keep his mind emptied, open to anything.

He found his little brother amid piles of dust, feathers like an eagle owl's, but larger, sprouted from his arms; and dense scales like a cobra's covered areas of his skin. When Tmra turned to look at him, Luxanthus saw that the right side of his face around his dark eye was edged by scales, the left side of his face around his orange eye edged by feathers. Aside from the scales and feathers, he was naked, his kilt having burned away in the flames he'd thrown himself into, and gold jewelry gone. The places the scales covered most densely were Tmra's neck, armpits, wrists, and inner thighs, a defense over the areas that would kill him quickest were he to be cut.

After a scan of his little brother's changed body—his fingernails were like talons, now, and his toenails as well—Luxanthus raised his gaze back to Tmra's smiling face and mismatched eyes, which with the snakelike scales and the owl-like feathers looked natural on him in a way they hadn't before.

"Tmra," Luxanthus greeted.

"Nkidu." His little brother smiled. It was a wild, giddy expression. "I can help you now." He raised one of his hands, fingers bent slightly to display the dark talons. "Anything that I scratch with all five fingers turns to dust. See?" He stepped up to a large glass statue of a leopard, dragging first one talon, then two, then three, then four, then finally five over the glass surface; as soon as he added the fifth finger, shockingly fast spiderwebbing cracks spread from Tmra's scratches throughout the rest of the statue, crumbling the entire thing to dust in a mere couple of seconds.

"It has to be all five fingers," Tmra said. The piles of dust covering the chamber said that he'd been experimenting. He looked back at Luxanthus, raising both of his taloned hands in front of him, bending and straightening his fingers. "But it's both hands. It works on both objects and people." He giggled, weak and shaky. "I disintegrated Mother."

Luxanthus looked back at him and willed his expression to remain unaffected. "I know," he said, maintaining a tone that was even and light.

Tmra smiled wider. "It doesn't work on me, though. See?" He raised a hand and drew red scratches over his cheek with all five talons of a hand. "I can scratch myself as much as I want." He scratched harder, so that beads of blood welled up.

Luxanthus's lips pressed together. "Please don't," he murmured, beseeching.

"Why not?" Tmra tilted his head, watching him, and scratched harder, smiling larger. "It feels good. Why does everyone always tell me to stop doing things that help?" His smile was wide, his eyes wider. "Scratching myself because I itch. Rubbing my eyes because they hurt. It helps." He laughed uncomprehendingly, distressedly. "So why shouldn't I?"

Luxanthus opened his mouth, then closed it again. He closed his eyes, then opened them again. "I'm sorry," he said lowly.

Tmra tilted his head further and smiled. "You didn't know, did you? It's okay. I forgive you." His eyes were wide and wild, but the curve of his lips had become soft. "Can you forgive me for disintegrating Mother?"

Luxanthus looked at him and exhaled softly. "You're forgiven," he said, meaning it. He'd never blamed his little brother for the things Tmra accidentally destroyed; nobody had. The boy had never meant to destroy anything, and he'd always been more torn up about it than anyone when it happened.

It was almost a shock to realize that even though Tmra had obviously undergone a drastic change, this kind of scenario wasn't exactly new.

"Say, Nkidu," Tmra said, looking down. He scratched the talons of his toenails over the floor, but it didn't disintegrate, so apparently the talons there didn't have the same power as those on his hands. "If we survive this, with all the Accursed"—he met Luxanthus's gaze with round eyes—"let's build a better temple to Silbalmu."

Then he smiled and reached out a hand, scratching all five talons over the wall of the temple.

The entire, great stone building completely disintegrated around them, making Luxanthus cover his mouth and cough from the dust flurries.

"…You don't think Silbalmu will be angry?" he asked, once he'd stopped coughing and could look back at his little brother, albeit with slightly watering eyes.

Tmra was twirling around in the dust with his lips pulled glee-fully away from his teeth and his feathered arms spread and stirring up a breeze. "I said we'd build a better one, didn't I?" he laughed. "If this gift Silbalmu gave me doesn't allow us to defeat the Accursed, then Silbalmu doesn't deserve a temple, anyway; if it does allow us to defeat the Accursed, then Silbalmu deserves a better one." The boy giggled, kicking a foot at the dust on the ground, sending it swirling into the air. "In either case, Silbalmu doesn't deserve *that* temple."

Luxanthus pressed his lips together, but let it go; there wasn't anything that could be done about it, so there was no point thinking on it. "It would be bad if you scratched something on accident," he said instead. He held out his hands, showing the strips of cloth. "Could you give me your hands, Tmra?" The boy looked at him with blank eyes, and Luxanthus said, "It's just a precaution."

He wasn't scared of what Tmra might do so much as he was

scared of what other people might do out of fear of the boy. Tmra had disintegrated an entire temple; people were going to be terrified. They needed to feel safe so they wouldn't do anything drastic.

Luxanthus looked at Tmra, a bit pleading.

Tmra stared back at him impassively for a moment, and then grinned. "Am I more dangerous than you now, Nkidu?" he asked as he skipped over, willingly holding out his hands, smile delighted but gaze sardonic. "Or just more uncontrollable?"

Luxanthus couldn't help the upward quirk of his lips, feeling somewhat droll. "Both," he said, taking his younger brother's taloned hands in his own and beginning to wrap the cloth carefully around and between the boy's fingers. "But you know what this means, right?" He looked up from his work to meet Tmra's gaze and smiled, feeling suddenly softer, his heart lighter. "If we work together, absolutely no one and nothing can stop us." He couldn't help but feel a bit delighted, realizing that he no longer had to wait for the Accursed to be defeated to spend time with his little brother again.

He stood up from where he'd been kneeling and ruffled his younger brother's hair, gently brushing his fingers over the tuft of mottled brown feathers that stuck up on the left side of the boy's head. "Let's reach even greater heights together, Tmra."

Tmra beamed in a way that made Luxanthus's soul soar. "If you throw me, I bet I could go really high," Tmra said, lifting up his feathered arms and cloth-wrapped hands, and Luxanthus obligingly picked the smaller boy up easily into his arms.

Luxanthus's eyes widened as he realized, "You're light." He looked at the boy in his arms, brow furrowing slightly, lips pressing together. "I mean, you were always light, but now you're even lighter." His eyes flicked over the feathers sprouting from his brother's skin, then back up to his face. "Are your bones hollow, now?" he asked.

Tmra smiled at him. "It would be hard to fly if they weren't, wouldn't it?"

"I suppose so," Luxanthus agreed. He adjusted his grip carefully around his little brother's naked but feather- and scale-covered body. "You'll have to be more careful not to break them, then."

"It's okay," Tmra said easily, wrapping his arms around Luxanthus's neck and leaning his head on his shoulder. "My body feels better, now." He stretched out a cloth-wrapped hand and hummed. "I think it'll finally actually listen to me."

Luxanthus blinked. "Your body didn't listen to you?" he asked, a little uncertainly. He couldn't imagine how that could be possible.

Tmra looked at him seriously and said, "It was worse than Naliki when Diyomendon tries to tell her to go away."

Luxanthus snorted, a surprised laugh vibrating his chest. "Okay," he admitted with a grin, "that was funny."

Tmra smiled back at him and brushed a cloth-wrapped hand over his cheek beneath his eye. "Now, though, I think my body will listen to me the way you do when I tell you to catch me," he said earnestly, and Luxanthus's lips pressed together.

"I might not always be there to catch you," he said quietly, unable to keep from frowning at the idea. It made his gut twist uncomfortably.

But Tmra held his gaze unwaveringly and said with utter assurance, "Yes, you will."

Luxanthus relaxed, lips curving upward. "Then if that's the case, the Accursed no longer stand a chance." Realizing that, he felt suddenly dazzlingly bright, and saw that same excited anticipation on his little brother's face. Luxanthus huffed, setting the boy back down.

"Fair is fair, though," he said, flicking at the boy's ear tuft and making Tmra wrinkle his nose and shake his head like it tickled. It made Luxanthus give a chuckle, but still he looked at his little brother seriously as he continued. "I had to go through some training first, so you do, too." At Tmra's horrified expression, Luxanthus added quickly, "Nowhere near as long. Not for years. We don't have that kind of time. But you have to go through some training before just heading out there." Tmra continued biting at his lower lip, obviously dissatisfied, and so Luxanthus flicked his ear tuft again and insisted, "Fair is fair."

Tmra let go of his lip with his teeth. "Okay," he relented.

Luxanthus smiled slightly. "Come on," he said, taking one of his little brother's cloth-wrapped hands and beginning to walk with him back to where their father and the guards were waiting. Luxanthus felt a trace of dread thinking about what that interaction and others following would bring, but brushed it aside. There was no point in worrying about it.

They'd get through it.

WHEN NALIKI HEARD the news that her little brother had thrown himself into the sacrificial fire in Silbalmu's Temple, gained the scales of a cobra, the feathers of an eagle owl, and a touch that decayed to dust anything he touched—and that he'd decayed their mother and then also the entire temple, but that Nkidu had led them both out alive—Naliki's mouth dropped open and her hands flew to it.

And then she burst out laughing. Because that was just—that was so *them*. That was so all of them. She could absolutely imagine her youngest brother doing something as crazy as jumping into a sacrificial fire; she could absolutely imagine her mother dying from hugging her own child; and she could absolutely imagine Nkidu walking out of it completely unscathed.

It was such an insane turn of events, and yet it made so much sense, and Naliki didn't know how to react to that but to laugh. She laughed until the tears streamed down her face, and she couldn't tell if it was just from the laughter or if she was also actually crying.

Then she turned to an unusually stoic Tdroki—he wasn't even silently raging and seething, which was another insane circumstance of the day that made sense, because none of them had ever been able to get mad at the ball of ridiculous endearment that was Tmra, no matter what he accidentally destroyed—and Naliki said, "It looks like I was right: Tmra would survive jumping off the roof."

If he'd survived jumping into a sacrificial fire. And now he had wings, to boot.

She grinned drolly at Tdroki, adding, "Which means that now, out of our siblings, it's only we two who would die."

"Luckily, we're also the two who would be smart enough to not jump off the roof," Tdroki said in return, and Naliki fell back into laughter.

Their father looked at them and said wryly, "I'm glad to see you're taking the news well"; and Naliki, whose laughter had subsided into giggles, giggled harder.

"How else are we supposed to take it?" she asked, and she'd thrown out her arms, grinning as she twirled herself dizzy and laughing. "Is there anyone alive at this point who hasn't gone a little insane?"

Months of being attacked by the Accursed every cursed night, of people being devoured and turned into monsters left and right, and it was either endure their existence in constant abject horror and terror or find humor and delight in the absurdity and morbidity.

And maybe hearing about the absolutely insane power that Rezekyrios had received made her giddy with the first trace of hope she'd felt in months that they might actually survive this.

Agamenjiyr looked at her tiredly and dispassionately, having survived by the alternate method of becoming completely emotionally numb to everything—rather understandably, since he was the king and had to bear the responsibility for it all, and there couldn't be any other way to bear such weight except to stop feeling it, like using fire to cauterize a wound—and Tdroki eerily echoed the vacant expression.

"You don't see us laughing like crazy people," Tdroki told her, tiredly and dispassionately, and she grinned at him with tears of laughter in her eyes and then started sobbing because he looked so, so much like a king.

V

THE KINGDOM OF ORDYUK was deteriorating: it was starting to feel more and more like Diyomendon's with each passing day. Because people's expectations were deteriorating, too.

Diyomendon didn't feel so angry anymore.

Ordyuk was falling apart, and the king could do nothing but watch. That was all Diyomendon had ever been able to do.

He watched the kingdom crumble and felt calm. Steady deterioration and eventual death was all life was, anyway. Finally, the truth of Diyomendon's reality was laid bare for everyone to see. No more false, glittering expectations.

How utterly fitting that Rezekyrios had gained a power to crumble everything even further away. The ability to turn humans, monsters, and entire kingdoms to dust.

"Good for Rezekyrios," Diyomendon said when he heard, something inside him settling, reassured and contented. "He finally made a place for himself."

Diyomendon didn't have to worry about his youngest brother, anymore.

REZEKYRIOS USED to lament at his every mistake, at everything he would accidentally break. Now, he completely destroyed everything he touched, and it was great.

Because now he was doing it on purpose.

The Accursed weren't scary, anymore. They turned to dust just like everything else. All it took was the slightest touch of the tips of his fingers, and they were gone. Something that delicate could never be scary.

Rezekyrios laughed as he ran through the streets destroying them, piles of dust blowing in the wind in his wake. It didn't matter if Rezekyrios could barely see in the dust and the dark; he was used to that, and he felt the monsters more than saw them. It didn't matter if they were behind him.

If any of the monsters might have impaled him, they were cut down by Nkidu. While Rezekyrios turned them to dust, Nkidu chopped off their heads, and that was fun because Rezekyrios could kick severed heads down the street ahead of him.

There wasn't anywhere the Accursed could get away from him, since the feathers on his arms allowed him to easily reach the roofs. And since he was always barefoot—scales on the bottoms of his feet rendered sandals unnecessary, and talons kept him from slipping or falling—he could feel the vibrations in the ground, letting him follow the monsters' movements even streets away.

Rezekyrios had a better sense of body temperature now, too. Even if the Accursed hid their insect and arachnid appendages, Rezekyrios could tell that they weren't human, because the appendages were large cold things curled inside their otherwise warm bodies. They couldn't trick him like they could Nkidu.

That had been difficult at first, because in the beginning Nkidu didn't always believe him. Nkidu had jumped in and prevented him from decaying one of the monsters, because it was a young girl and he thought she was human. Only, then she'd attacked Nkidu when his back was turned, and he would have been killed if Rezekyrios hadn't reached out a hand to catch her scorpion-like appendage and turn her to dust.

Nkidu had stopped doubting him, after that.

"Did I do well, Nkidu?" Rezekyrios would ask.

"Yes, Tmra," Nkidu would say, hands interlaced with his, holding his fingers so that the talons couldn't touch him. "You did very well. Countless lives of both civilians and soldiers are being saved because of you."

There would be dust in Rezekyrios's mouth, and he would smile. "I'm glad."

IT WAS AN UNDENIABLE FACT that the future of Ordyuk had become much brighter since Rezekyrios had become a Blessed Warrior.

Agamenjiyr, though, was still tired, and was only growing progressively more so. That was another undeniable fact.

Yet another undeniable fact was that Agamenjiyr's father, the previous king, had also become a Blessed Warrior. He hadn't survived the Great Calamity, and it wasn't the Accursed that had killed him; it had been the same Blessing that allowed him to fight. For the other Blessed Warriors, it had been the same, though some survived with their powers longer than others. But none of them had lived more than a few years after receiving their Blessings; the incredible powers the Daimmu granted them ate away their lives too quickly. Agamenjiyr expected the same fate for his youngest son.

Rezekyrios was the happiest anyone had ever seen him. The boy's birth hadn't been planned, but Agamenjiyr couldn't help but think that perhaps Akukele, Daimu of Fate, had intended the boy for this exact purpose. That it was the reason for the boy's different-colored eyes, for the fact that he'd never seemed comfortable in his skin; the fact that he'd always been so prone to destroying things.

Agamenjiyr couldn't lament any of it, seeing the way the boy had come so much into his own.

Rezekyrios wasn't the only one, though. Luxanthus had seemed at complete peace with himself ever since he'd been allowed to fight the Accursed each night, and Diyomendon had seemed to grow more confident and certain of himself as heir the more the kingdom deteriorated. If there was any king who wouldn't suffer the aftermath of another Great Calamity but would instead flourish, it was Diyomendon.

Even Naliki seemed to have been born to flourish in such dark times, laughing as she always did at everything, seeming to draw strength from others' pain. In circumstances where anyone else would break, Agamenjiyr's children grew strong. In them, he saw a future for Ordyuk.

Like a goal that had finally come into sight, these things gave Agamenjiyr the strength to push on, to continue to defy the exhaustion trying to bring him to his knees.

When he died, it would be on his feet, standing tall as a king. Just as he'd been born to be.

His son Rezekyrios was hardly alone in the fate of dying under the curse of the incredible power he'd been blessed with—and Agamenjiyr refused to pity him just like he'd always refused to pity himself.

LUXANTHUS HAD CONFLICTING feelings regarding his little brother's Blessing. Some things were more enjoyable, now—other things less so. He didn't make a habit of dwelling on it; after all, that was how life was. He simply took mental note of it and then filed the information away to draw upon only when it was useful.

Some of the developments were puzzling, though.

Tmra was always scratching at himself, now. He'd scratch himself to bleeding with his talons—or, if his hands were wrapped up, he'd rub his skin raw on available surfaces like a cat rubbing against someone's legs.

"It's itchy," he'd say, giggling even as he bled. "It's so itchy."

The only time he stopped trying to scratch at himself was when he was actively disintegrating things. It was hard to tell if he actually stopped feeling itchy at those times, or if he was simply too preoccupied to scratch.

Tmra wasn't exactly more graceful than he used to be, but he made his awkwardness work. It made him a challenge to fight, because he always seemed a beat or two off—either too fast or too slow—or his movements would be entirely unpredictable as he almost strategically tripped over his feet or flailed and knocked into something. He dodged the Accursed's arachnid appendages with such unfailing ease that it seemed purposeful; and yet the way he did made the entire thing look like one huge, serendipitous accident.

Luxanthus found it a challenge, too, when he had to subdue his brother. Which he had to do at the end of each night, to keep Tmra from continuing to rampage. Tmra would start each night relatively controlled, but by the approach of dawn, he'd be practically crazed, disintegrating things with reckless abandon and laughing madly. Luxanthus would have to pin him down and grab his hands with a towel so he couldn't touch anything.

Tmra's face would be pressed down against the dirt, but he'd turn his head enough to grin up at him. "Did I do well, Nkidu?"

"Yes, Tmra," Luxanthus would say, holding the squirming boy immobile. "You did very well. Countless lives of both civilians and soldiers are being saved because of you."

Tmra's mismatched eyes would be bright as he'd say, "I'm glad," but his smile was always wild and insensible.

The younger boy didn't ever seem to hold it against him, even as Luxanthus cut off his breath until he finally passed out before carrying him back to the palace.

Luxanthus didn't particularly enjoy that part.

He did enjoy most of the rest, though. He truly enjoyed fighting the Accursed alongside Tmra: fighting and spending time with his little brother being the two things that made him feel the most content. Getting to do those two things together was fun. Teaming up with Tmra was easy, and also thrilling.

When he threw his little brother into the air now, the boy could indeed reach incredibly high.

Some of it did disturb him sometimes, and it was more than the matter of his little brother's questionable sanity. Tmra also seemed to have acquired a way of sensing whether someone was Accursed, and it was unsettling to see people who'd looked like normal civilians—especially young children and the elderly—revealed as monsters. It made Luxanthus wonder how long some of them had been Accursed, blending in with human society.

Luxanthus avoided thinking about it. Questioning the matter wouldn't change anything. The answers, had they been known, wouldn't have changed anything either. Luxanthus's duty was defend the people of Ordyuk and kill the Accursed. If his feelings were conflicted, that wasn't any different from before. He'd always had conflicted feelings about things, and had always ignored that, because it didn't matter. That hadn't changed.

The only real difference was that now he was fighting alongside his little brother; and with Tmra's ability to decay whatever he touched, they were able to hold the monster attacks off much better than before.

"Did I do well, Nkidu?" Tmra asked at the end of each night, looking up at him with a crazed, endearing smile.

And each night, Luxanthus's lips curved in return, even as he held his little brother down and slowly constricted his breath, and answered honestly, "Yes, Tmra. You did very well."

NALIKI FOUND Tmra a lot easier to interact with, now that he was Blessed.

He wasn't scared of her anymore.

He used to be scared of everything, and even the smallest things would affect him. Now he truly didn't seem to be scared of or bothered by anything.

He spent the nights fighting the Accursed with Nkidu; but during the day he was kept in a cage, his deadly hands wrapped up and a collar around his neck attached to a chain connected to the floor.

Tmra seemed to find it funny.

"I don't have to be scared anymore," Tmra told her. He gestured with his wrapped hands to the cage, the collar, the chain, and then grinned and said, "It's like I'm the scariest thing out there!"

Naliki smirked and said, "I'm not scared of you."

Tmra's lips curved slyly as he held out his hands, taunting with a glint in his eye, "Unwrap them, then."

"I'm also not an idiot," Naliki snorted, a hand on her hip, and Tmra giggled.

Naliki liked visiting him like this.

"Hey, Tmra," she greeted, picking the lock of the cage and letting herself in just like she'd always entered Tdroki's locked room; and just like with Tdroki, she locked the door behind her, and turned around with a grin.

"Rkalla," Tmra greeted, smiling at her.

He actually, genuinely smiled at her, now.

Naliki loved it.

She grinned in return. "I brought you something," she said, and Tmra looked at the item she was carrying and snorted.

"It's always honey cake, with you," he noted, lips twitching slightly as she unwrapped the dessert.

"What can I say?" she said saccharinely, holding up the small cake like a treat to a dog. "I'm just that sweet."

Tmra rolled his two different-colored eyes, but smirked slightly and said, "Thanks," as he took a bite out of the cake she was holding, eating it from her hands like a dog instead of holding it in his awkwardly wrapped hands. He even barked at her, and she snorted.

"How's it been going out there?" she asked him, once he was done. He'd tried to lick her fingers once, but she'd shoved him lightly and said, "Eww, no," and he'd giggled but sat obediently back.

He regarded her curiously. "You haven't asked Nkidu?" he wanted to know.

Naliki snorted and waved her hand. "Oh, I ask him," she said, "but he always just gives me that blank expression of his and says, 'It's fine. Accursed are dying, and I haven't yet.'" She made a face and Tmra's lips quirked.

"Not inaccurate," he pointed out, and Naliki stuck her tongue out at him.

"Boring, though," she said, and added slyly, "I was hoping I'd get a more interesting answer out of you."

Tmra blinked at her with his cobra- and owl-like eyes, and then looked away, suddenly sober and thoughtful. The abrupt change of mood took Naliki aback.

"'Interesting,' huh," the young boy mused. "Silbalmu said that, too." He met her gaze again. "That the things I do should be interesting."

Naliki hadn't heard that. "That so?" she prompted, curiosity piqued.

Tmra hummed. "I've been contemplating that: what makes something interesting or not. Is it just when things are unexpected, or—?" He was looking at her searchingly. "What makes something 'interesting' for you, Rkalla?"

Naliki hummed in return; she hadn't given it much thought, before. "When things are unexpected, certainly," she agreed. She tilted her head, pursing her lips. "But not only that, I guess. I mean, Tdroki's anger is always interesting, even though it's always expected. So things are interesting when they're exciting and different, I guess. It doesn't necessarily have to be entirely unexpected, just…slightly different. Not always the same exact thing."

She tapped her fingers over the floor. "I guess the problem with Nkidu is that he's so good at everything that he's able to do everything exactly the same each time, 'cause he does everything absolutely perfectly each time." She shrugged, then, concluding, "So I guess imperfections are interesting."

Tmra laughed. "Well, in that case I suppose I don't have to worry about it." He grinned at her, black and yellow-orange eyes bright and widening ever so slightly larger. "I'll be interesting without even having to try."

"I certainly would never have counted 'boring' as being among your flaws," she agreed, teasingly.

By the Daimmu, she loved him so much more now that he wasn't scared of her.

He nodded easily in concurrence, diverted as he raised an arm under the chain attached to the collar around his neck, lifting the metal links close to his face and beginning to rub his scaled cheek against it.

Naliki huffed. "You look like a cat," she said, raising an eyebrow at him.

"Last time I checked I had both scales and feathers, but no fur," he informed her dryly, letting the chain down and then lying on top of it, rolling it between his spine and shoulder blade, first on one side and then on the other. He was making a disgruntled face, nose wrinkling and lip curling in displeasure, and Naliki snorted at him.

"It's the way you're rubbing yourself like that," she said, gesturing at him pointedly.

"I'm itchy," he said, petulant. "I'm itchy all over." Then he turned his head to look at her, eyes slightly wild as he grinned. "It's maddening."

Such displays had become typical of him since becoming Blessed, and Naliki huffed again and held out a hand, flexing and straightening her fingers pointedly. "Well, come on over." When he crawled over, she began scratching his back with her nails, focusing on the skin at the edges of the patches of scales and feathers. "How's that?" she asked.

"That feels good." Tmra practically melted over her crossed legs, eyes fluttering half-closed. Lowly and contentedly, he murmured, "Thanks."

Naliki smiled at him and kept scratching. "Of course," she said.

IT WAS ONLY LATE AFTERNOON, but Rezekyrios was already awake when Diyomendon entered the building at the outskirts of the gardens where he was being kept.

"Rezekyrios," Diyomendon greeted.

The chained Silbalmu-Blessed smiled up at him. "Diyomendon."

Diyomendon unlocked the cage door and stepped inside. "Come on." He walked over and unlocked the collar around Rezekyrios's neck, letting the metal drop unceremoniously to the floor. "I need your help with something."

Rezekyrios glanced down at the discarded collar and chain, and then back up at him. "Are you supposed to be doing this?"

Diyomendon took his little brother's hands, beginning to unwrap the cloth that was so crudely and thickly wrapped around them. "I'm going to be the next king," he said. He tossed the wrappings aside, Rezekyrios's taloned hands now freed. "I can do whatever I want."

Rezekyrios looked down at his hands, flexing and straightening his taloned fingers, and then looked up at Diyomendon again, tilting his head. "You're really not scared of me at all."

Diyomendon looked down at him, unimpressed. "Why should I be?" He turned to leave, knowing that his brother would follow him.

He heard Rezekyrios giggle behind him. "There are scarier things inside of you, aren't there?"

Diyomendon's lips quirked ever so slightly as he kept walking. "You've always seen things that nobody else does." He glanced back over his shoulder, meeting the black and yellow-orange gaze framed by scales and feathers. "It's nice to see you finally so comfortable with yourself, Rezekyrios."

The Silbalmu-Blessed looked back at him easily. "What do you need me to do?"

Diyomendon grinned at him, dark hot flames flickering in his chest. "To help me destroy some things."

Rezekyrios laughed. "That is indeed what I'm best at, isn't it?"

Diyomendon looked back ahead of him, continuing to walk. "What can I say? It's a king's job to use his subordinates to the best of their abilities."

Quietly, Rezekyrios said, "It's nice to see you finally so comfortable with yourself, too, Diyomendon."

Diyomendon glanced back at him, saw his younger brother looking at him, solemn and unflinching. He huffed, reaching out to shove the boy lightly in the head. "No speaking out of turn, subordinate."

He kept walking, and Rezekyrios giggled behind him, following close like a shadow.

TRIP, STUMBLE, FALL; jump, glide, decay—the world was a wondrous place, and Rezekyrios had never been happier.

He'd never seen Nkidu, Rkalla, or Diyomendon happier.

Turn, flip, slice; laugh, taunt, tease; glare, grin, burn. The world was a wondrous place. The days were filled with bustle and music, the nights filled with fire and screams. Both the sunlight and the darkness were blinding, but Rezekyrios's eyes didn't ache anymore.

He did itch, though. His skin itched maddeningly. He liked how good it felt when he scratched it.

The only time his skin didn't itch was when the world was turning to dust at his fingertips. He liked the dry taste of the dust, and the soft sound of its falling. He liked watching the bright and dark specks dance lightly in the air and fall gently from the sky.

He liked watching Nkidu fight the way a bird sang: like all was right in the world. It felt like it was.

He liked seeing the fear in the Accursed's eyes as their bodies decayed to dust. He liked watching them blow away, like nightmares disintegrating in the light of day. He liked laughing without feeling afraid.

He liked the tastes of blood-saturated meat and honey-saturated cake. He liked the sound of the metal chain brushing over the floor as he paced, and the creak of the cage door when it was opened. He liked the hush that came over the Ordyukian warriors when he came out holding Nkidu's hand, touching Nkidu with all five of his fingers and four of his claws. He liked the way his brothers and sister weren't afraid he'd turn them to dust even though he'd disintegrated their mother.

He liked listening to Rkalla talk like a kitten pounced on toes. He liked seeing Diyomendon move like a fire through dry shrub and King Agamenjiyr move like he was above the horizon. He liked the way his father looked at him like he was reassuring. He liked the way everyone smiled at him like he was colluder to their deepest, darkest, most delightful and sinister secrets.

He liked feeling the sunlight warm his scales; liked feeling the breeze ruffle his feathers; liked feeling the world catch beneath the talons on his toes and crumble beneath the talons on his fingers.

He liked that the world could be so wondrous while the kingdom was being attacked nightly by monsters and people were constantly dying. He liked that the world could be so wondrous even as he helped destroy it, and both humans and monsters looked at him like he was scary.

Rezekyrios scratched at his maddeningly itching skin and smiled at how good it felt when he drew blood.

He thought that the world was a wondrous place, and he liked that it didn't seem like it would ever end, no matter what crumbled to dust or who died.

VI

AGAMENJIYR SHOULD HAVE expected it, really: that King Morphioce of the Kingdom of Mythus would invade Ordyuk to annex it to the Mythusian Empire.

Morphioce had always been willing to do anything to accomplish his goals. No matter what sacrifices had to be made, personal or otherwise. No matter what he had to destroy or whom he had to kill.

Between the kings of the other three kingdoms—Chansa to the west, Hahsin to the north, and Mythus to the northwest—Agamenjiyr had always liked Morphioce of Mythus best. Unlike the puerile and vacuous Feliyama of Chansa or the boisterous and obnoxious Tsander of Hahsin, Morphioce was serious, self-possessed, and pleasurable to negotiate with. Ordyuk and Mythus had always been on good terms, despite their nearly opposite views regarding the deities.

Given the situation with the Accursed, it was no surprise that Morphioce had made his move. He'd always been a forelooking individual; Agamenjiyr didn't doubt that the King of Mythus had been preparing for the return of the Accursed since the moment he'd taken the Mythusian throne as a child after the Great Calamity.

Agamenjiyr allowed the troops of the Mythusian Army to march through the streets of Ordyuk to the palace without resistance. Ordyuk was weak and ravaged by the Accursed; the kingdom was in no position to fight against the powerhouse that was Mythus.

Even if Ordyuk had been strong enough, there would never have been any sense in going to war against a man like Morphioce.

When the King of Mythus and his men entered the throne room, Agamenjiyr rose from his throne to meet him, the two of them meeting in the center of the floor with their men gestured to remain back. They looked at each other, Agamenjiyr slightly taller and more muscular, Morphioce keeping his perpetual blank expression.

Morphioce was stunning, as he always was. Skin only a shade darker than the cream white of his tunic, hair an entire shade lighter, and eyes the intense blue of the hottest part of flame. His crown was a simple gold circlet ringed with small sapphires.

Agamenjiyr was tired. He looked down at the other king and refused the urge to close his eyes. "I won't fight you, Morphioce." He lifted his chin. "But I also won't kneel."

There was the faintest suggestion of a smile on Morphioce's otherwise blank face. "As I would expect of you, Agamenjiyr."

They both knew how this was going to go.

Morphioce glanced idly around the hall. "I must say, though: Ordyuk has fared better under the Accursed attacks than I would have suspected, considering how unprepared you were." His stare returned to Agamenjiyr's, misleadingly indolent. "You should have listened when I told you they would return."

Agamenjiyr didn't answer. He held the other man's gaze, refusing to close his eyes.

Morphioce had always been telling him and the other two kings that the Accursed would return and that they should prepare for them; Agamenjiyr had always prioritized the welfare of his people over uncertain eventualities. He did not regret the way he had ruled. Morphioce may have prepared for the reappearance of the Accursed, but the standard of living in Mythus was far lower than in Ordyuk as a consequence.

Morphioce made a show of giving a put-upon sigh. "How have you been holding them off?"

"Highly skilled warriors," Agamenjiyr said simply, because there was no point in trying to deny a man like Morphioce the answers he wanted. If you refused to give him what he asked, he had no qualms about taking it by force.

Morphioce's face remained expressionless, his eyebrows rising without emotion. "That's admirable. All of them human, or do you have warriors who have received blessings from the Daimmu you've always trusted so much?"

Mythus had, since Morphioce had taken the throne, been known by the other three kingdoms as the Nullifidian Kingdom. Its temples had long been destroyed and all manner of worship to the Daimmu abolished. It was one of the relatively few matters on which Agamenjiyr and Morphioce had never agreed.

Agamenjiyr was tired, but he held Morphioce's gaze. "We have a few who are Blessed."

Flame-blue eyes burned hot in an innocuous face. "Not enough, it seems. Though I suppose you must feel awfully pleased, believing that your deities haven't completely abandoned you."

Agamenjiyr was tired. He straightened his shoulders beneath the weight of the sky and smiled slightly. "We worship the Daimmu, but we have never held them responsible for making our lives facile; an unchallenging life is not one worth living."

He'd always greatly respected Morphioce's intelligence. There were some ways, though, that he'd always thought the other man a hopeless child, angry at his parents for being unable to protect him from the world.

He and Morphioce were, both of them, trapped in that fateful day of the Great Calamity all those years ago, when they were forced onto thrones too large for them with entire monster-ravaged countries at their feet. They were almost the same age, and among the four kings, there'd always been a kind of solidarity between the two of them—one that wasn't shared by Feliyama, who'd been too young at the time to remember the disaster at all, or Tsander, who'd been old enough that he'd partaken in the Great Calamity as a warrior and emerged in the aftermath as a hero.

There'd always been an understanding between the two of them, and Agamenjiyr had never felt it as keenly as he did then, as Morphioce stepped closer to him and looked at him with something almost like readable emotion.

"I always liked you, Agamenjiyr." He took Agamenjiyr's chin in his hand, turning his head slightly. "But by those Daimmu that you hold so dear, you look like shit. When was the last time you slept?"

Agamenjiyr couldn't remember. He looked at Morphioce without answering.

Morphioce clicked his tongue. "That long, huh." He removed his fingers from Agamenjiyr's face, reaching down to his belt and the scabbard at his hip. "Well, now you'll finally get to." He pulled out the sword with a graceful flourish, held it gently with both hands in front of him. The thin blade glinted as he tilted it slightly. The handle was austere and practical, like Morphioce himself. "I had this sword specially fashioned and sharpened by the finest swordsmith in Mythus. You won't feel a thing."

He grasped the sword firmly by the hilt and swung it up, pausing it next to Agamenjiyr's neck, flame-blue eyes flickering over his face. "Get some much-deserved rest, you cursed, sedulous king."

"Hypocrite," said Agamenjiyr softly.

"You are the only person I will ever allow to call me that," Morphioce said as he pulled back the sword. "Do me a favor and stay dead."

Morphioce hadn't lied about the blade: Agamenjiyr didn't feel a thing before he was simply gone, as if he'd finally, finally fallen asleep.

THE ENTIRE SCENE had been like a dream. The King of Mythus had entered the hall with his metal-armored warriors; he and King Agamenjiyr had conversed in the center of the floor like close acquaintances; and then the King of Mythus had sliced off Agamenjiyr's head.

To the eyes of most, the movement had probably been too fast to comprehend; Luxanthus, though, being highly trained with blades and having honed his reflexes to a razor edge, saw clearly the blade's smooth, skilled arc, and the way the King of Mythus had already been moving to catch Agamenjiyr's head before its trajectory even began.

The King of Mythus caught first Agamenjiyr's head, and then Agamenjiyr's body as it slumped. The blood from the severed neck gushed over the King of Mythus's pale skin and clothes as he gently laid the body of the Ordyukian king down, positioned his head back above his neck, and closed his eyes with pointer and ring finger.

"There," said the King of Mythus as he did. "Now you can sleep."

Then he stood, stained glistening scarlet with the King of Ordyuk's blood, and looked at where Luxanthus, Diyomendon, and Rkalla were standing by the vacant throne.

"Well," the King of Mythus said, expression blank and tone brusque, "it looks like Ordyuk is part of the Mythusian Empire, now. We'll have to negotiate the terms." He pulled out a pale handkerchief, wiping the blood from his hands. "We're not asking for much." His strikingly blue gaze landed on Diyomendon. "You're the crown prince, right? You can still be the sovereign who makes most of the decisions regarding Ordyuk affairs, as long as you obey any instructions you receive. I'll need to know that you'll obey, though." His gaze slid over Rkalla and Luxanthus. "Give me one of your younger siblings to assure your loyalty," he said, and looked back at Diyomendon. "You can choose which."

Diyomendon was trembling, fists clenched at his sides. Rkalla had a hand on his shoulder and moved closer to him.

Luxanthus stepped forward. "I'll go," he said.

It had to be him. It couldn't be Rkalla, as she was the only princess, as well as being the only one who could deal with Diyomendon's anger. And it certainly couldn't be Tmra, who'd been hidden as soon as the Mythusian Army entered the city, and who was an even greater weapon against the Accursed than Luxanthus.

It had to be him. From the way Diyomendon was trembling silently and Rkalla had bowed her head slightly, they obviously knew it, too.

"Fine by me," the King of Mythus said carelessly. He gestured to his guards. "Take him."

Luxanthus walked over toward them and they met him near the center of the hall, grabbing him harshly and wrenching his arms behind his back to restrain him, shoving his head down. "You don't have to be rough," Luxanthus said quietly. "I won't fight."

"Listen to him," dictated the King of Mythus. "He's a prince and the son of a respected colleague. Do treat him accordingly."

The men let up his head and lightened their grips, leading rather than shoving him out of the hall. The King of Mythus's blue eyes followed them for a moment and then turned back to Diyomendon.

As Luxanthus passed his dead father lying on the floor, he saw that, even against the spreading puddle of blood over the stone, the man who had been king looked peaceful.

THEY WATCHED THEIR father be slain and then their younger brother led away, Tdroki trembling violently beneath her fingers as Naliki held on to him to keep herself steady.

It was so reassuring the way he was shaking.

As long as Tdroki was still angry, the world wasn't ending. The world couldn't end; an angry Tdroki would never let it.

Naliki propped herself up on that as the King of Mythus approached them, his strange washed-out lightness drenched in the vivid red of their father's blood. The man's expression was cold and utterly unfeeling, yet when he'd caught Agamenjiyr's head and body and laid the dead man on the floor, it had been so tenderly.

Naliki fought back shivers. She couldn't help but wonder, not without some amount of fear, what this man wanted so badly that he was willing to kill someone whom he didn't want to let fall.

The man looked at Tdroki with his cold blue eyes, aloof and brusque. "All right. You're crowned head of Ordyuk as a province of the Mythusian Empire. Let's negotiate the terms and requirements."

Tdroki shook. The King of Mythus continued uncaringly, "The first is that I be given a room in the palace for the duration of my stay, and the washroom better be excellent." He looked at them with eyes that had Agamenjiyr's blood darkening their pale eyelashes and flecking their corners like dark glitter. "We can negotiate the rest after I bathe and change, as I'm sure none of us want to undertake the task with me covered in your former king's blood."

He stank of the blood saturating his clothes, and it made Naliki feel nauseous.

"Let go of me, Naliki," Tdroki said, angry and quiet as he pulled his arm from her grip.

Naliki forced a smile onto her face, turning her gaze to the King of Mythus. "I can show you to a room, Your Liege," she said, not entirely sure why. All she knew was that the man himself wasn't what scared her; she wasn't scared of him.

He looked at her expressionlessly, with eyes blue like the faint steady hearts of flame. "That would be appreciated."

Tdroki looked at her sharply, with eyes red-orange like wild flickering flame-tongues. "Naliki."

It made Naliki laugh absurdly, seeing them both look at her like that. "Relax." She smiled at her brother, not altogether without mockery. "You can entrust the sovereign of our empire with me. I'll behave myself, I promise." She looked at the King of Mythus, smiled not altogether without wryness, and said, "If you would follow me, Your Liege."

She turned and left, the King of Mythus's steps following behind her. She didn't turn to look at him; her father was dead, one of her younger brothers was gone, and it felt like sharp shards of glass were embedded in her chest and bleeding. But when she looked at the King of Mythus, she couldn't shake away the mental image of a heart impaled from so many directions that it had become like a bloodless, glittering ornament.

The Accursed would be back again that night.

They were walking through the halls, and the King of Mythus asked coolly, "Was Agamenjiyr that terrible of a father that you're happy at his passing, or is this a sickeningly obsequious act?"

Naliki couldn't help it: she laughed at him. "No, I loved my father. But I've been prepared to lose everyone. I've already lost my mother and youngest brother to the conflict with the Accursed." They'd let Tmra out of his cage earlier that day and told him to hide. The official story was that he was dead; they couldn't let the Mythusians know about him. "I don't know if any of us will survive." The shards of glass in Naliki's chest hurt terribly, and she laughed and blinked away the tears that tried to bead in her eyes. "I laugh and smile so I don't break," she told the man who'd killed her father and taken her brother. "What else am I supposed to do? Drown myself in tears?"

"That strength is admirable." The steps of the King of Mythus behind her didn't falter. "I suppose I shouldn't expect anything less from Agamenjiyr's daughter." His voice was void of feeling, bordering on derision if anything at all, but there was unmistakable respect in his words, and Naliki couldn't help but remember the way the two men had spoken to each other and the way the King of Mythus had caught Agamenjiyr's head and body so he didn't crumple gracelessly to the floor.

"You seemed close," Naliki said, quietly. She didn't turn to look at him.

Coldly, the man replied, "You seem truly impertinent."

That was as good an admittance as any. "My father always did tell me that tendency of mine would get me in trouble one day," she said. She finally turned to look at the foreign king as she pulled up to one of the chambers reserved for high-ranking guests. She bowed her head slightly, gesturing. "Your room, Your Liege."

The man's blood-flecked expression was unreadable. "I assume the room is equipped with fresh garments."

"Not necessarily ones to your liking," Naliki said. The room of course contained Ordyukian clothing, but nothing like the tunic and trousers the Mythusian King was wearing.

"It'll be fine, as long as they're clean and of good quality," the man said dismissively, brushing past her to enter the chamber. "Your presence here is no longer required. Make yourself scarce." He disappeared into the room and shut the door firmly. In a display of uncaring self-assurance, he didn't bother to lock the door.

All the glass shards in Naliki's chest were digging in painfully and bloodily, and she turned and walked away, humming to try to keep herself from falling apart. As she did, she wondered how much more it would take before her heart, like that of the King of Mythus, became like an ornament: glittering and absolutely bloodless.

KING MORPHIOCE OF MYTHUS entered the study washed of King Agamenjiyr's blood, wearing an embroidered Ordyukian kilt. He was barefoot, and the only jewelry he was wearing was the gold circlet of a crown around his head. The kilt exposed the dark scars that littered his legs and torso. He looked utterly uncaring about any of it.

He sat down at the table and pushed a scroll across the table to Diyomendon. "Here are the terms. You have no choice but to accept."

Diyomendon took the scroll and read it thoroughly, not particularly surprised by any of it.

There wasn't much that the Kingdom of Mythus could possibly want or demand from the Accursed-ravaged Ordyuk, aside from those experiences dealing with the Accursed and the experimental ground they provided for anti-Accursed strategies. Diyomendon, as the crown prince, had been the confidant of his father and king: he was well aware that preparing to fight against the Accursed had been the priority of the King of Mythus's entire reign, and that Ordyuk was to become the practice ground for the strategies that would eventually be used to protect Mythus.

Reading the contract revealed that, in essence, it would be Diyomendon's role to take care of all the affairs of Ordyuk save those involving direct conflict with the Accursed, which would be in the hands of the occupying Mythusian Army. Fighting the Accursed was all that Mythus truly cared about.

Diyomendon was not surprised by this. He had also not been surprised by his father's death, and had recognized that it was an altogether incredibly benevolent show of Morphioce's respect for the other king. What had so severely angered him was the King of Mythus's demand for one of his siblings; he'd understood the political necessity of the demand, and the point that Morphioce was making that he did not trust Diyomendon like he had trusted Agamenjiyr, but it killed Diyomendon all the same.

By the Daimmu, his siblings were *his*, and he hated the emotional leverage that the King of Mythus was holding over him.

He hated that it was the exact technique he would have used in Morphioce's place.

He'd understood why Luxanthus had stepped forward of his own accord—they all knew that it could only have been Luxanthus.

Diyomendon couldn't decide if he was grateful to his brother for offering himself so that he hadn't had to, or if he hated him for protecting him like that.

Luxanthus had always been so utterly perfect.

Diyomendon didn't know if Ordyuk was better off now or not. If an entire brigade of the Mythusian Army was compensation enough for the loss of the Daimmu-Blessed Luxanthus, and the fact that Rezekyrios was forced into hiding.

There was no telling what a man like Morphioce would do with the incredible power of the feathered and scaled boy, were he to know about him.

Diyomendon glanced up from the document to look at the King of Mythus, who was watching him with a blank, bored-looking expression, and then Diyomendon signed and stamped his agreement to the terms.

As Morphioce had said, he didn't have a choice. And altogether, as far as the Kingdom of Ordyuk was concerned, it was for the best. They would have the protection of the Mythusian Army, which would be sincerely doing its best to battle the Accursed; and in return, Mythus demanded only complete authority to defend Ordyuk in any way it wished. Mythus gained nothing except for a practice arena. It would have seemed sickeningly kind, if it weren't so clear that King Morphioce, despite his relationship with Agamenjiyr, didn't care about Ordyuk at all—that that was the only reason why Diyomendon would be left with all the affairs not concerned with battling the Accursed.

Diyomendon understood the entire arrangement perfectly, and he hated the King of Mythus for it in the same way he'd always hated Luxanthus: for the fact that there was nothing that he could truly hate him for. King Morphioce of Mythus even shared Luxan-thus's utterly blank expression and inflectionless tone.

Diyomendon hated them both. Maybe it was best that Luxan-thus ended up under the King of Mythus's thumb. Diyomendon wondered what Morphioce would do with the Daimmu-Blessed warrior. He didn't care. He had Naliki—nothing would ever be able to pry Naliki from him—and he had Rezekyrios, if the latter only in secret.

Rezekyrios had always been the best at keeping secrets; ironic that he should become one himself.

Diyomendon wasn't sure whether to feel empowered or power-less under King Morphioce's terms. He settled on simply feeling angry. It made his signature bold and deep, and there was a certain amount of satisfaction in that.

He passed the signed-and-stamped scroll back, and King Morphioce rolled it up, handed it to one of his men, and stood. "A pleasure negotiating with you, Nobilissimus Diyomendon. I hope this is the beginning of a long and mutually beneficial relationship."

"Only if we're both lucky," Diyomendon returned; and when King Morphioce left the room laughing, his own Mythusian men looked disturbed.

The Ordyukian guards and officials who were present, being well-used to untoward laughter, were not disturbed in the least.

IT HAD BEEN midmorning when Diyomendon had shown up, unlocked the cage door and then Rezekyrios's collar, though he'd left Rezekyrios's hands wrapped as he'd pushed him outside.

"The Mythusian Army is here," Diyomendon had said. "They're going to take Ordyuk under their jurisdiction." He'd given Rezekyr-ios another push. "Get out of here. They can't know about you. They can't see you. They can't find you. Go hide in the desert. You should be able to survive just fine, the way you are now."

Rezekyrios had looked at him and grinned. "What does this mean?"

"It means that now you have to kill the Accursed outside of the city instead of inside it," Diyomendon had told him, looking at him seriously; angrily. "No matter what, do not let any of the Mythusian warriors see you."

Rezekyrios had grinned wider. "So I'm Ordyuk's secret, now?"

Diyomendon had grinned sharply, connivingly, back at him. "Exactly."

Rezekyrios had left giggling, running snake-fast over the ground and then jumping and flapping owl-silent over the walls, out into the desert where the rest of Silbalmu's creatures lived.

Now he was truly one of them.

IT WAS ONLY once the King of Mythus was departing Ordyuk along with his officials, leaving most of his warriors behind to occupy the kingdom that was now a province of the Mythusian Empire, that Luxanthus saw King Morphioce again.

"Can I ask what you're going to do with me?" he inquired from his seat next to the king.

Luxanthus was not bound in any way, but the other man was utterly relaxed next to him, seeming as comfortable in an Ordyukian kilt as he'd been in his Mythusian tunic and trousers.

"You've gotten used to fighting those Accursed, haven't you?" the man said, looking at him with eyes that were a color like Luxanthus had never seen.

Luxanthus nodded.

The King of the Mythusian Empire waved a hand. "We'll have you fight some for us. Are you familiar with the concept of gladiator games?"

Luxanthus shook his head.

"It shouldn't be that different from the life you were living,"

King Morphioce said, shrugging. He looked at Luxanthus with intensely blue, unreadable eyes. "All you have to do is kill your opponents before they kill you."

Luxanthus's lips quirked. "Yes," he agreed, "that does sound the same."

He'd probably never see Ordyuk again—and it probably wouldn't matter.

NALIKI FOUND THAT life under Mythusian rule wasn't that different from how it had been before, all things considered.

King Agamenjiyr might not have been there anymore, but Tdroki's presence was just as strong and reassuring in its own way. Nkidu and Tmra might not have been there anymore to fight the Accursed each night, but the Mythusian Army was proving as effective a defense against the Accursed, if not more so. The nights were filled with less screaming.

The days, though, were also filled with less music, less art, and less dancing; the presence of the Mythusian Army brought more safety, but also a more somber and stifled atmosphere. It was a strange paradox to have to reconcile: that the atmosphere of the kingdom had been brighter when it had been more filled with death; that safety did not equal happiness; that greater danger had brought about so much more celebration.

Things were not so bad, though. Fewer people were dying. That was undeniably a good thing. People were able to live their lives almost entirely normally, despite the nightly monster attacks. Altogether, perhaps life had returned more to how it was before the Accursed appeared. It was hard to remember, though.

Naliki, for her part, was mostly just lonelier.

Now that Tdroki was essentially the king, he had even less time for her, and there was no Tmra to visit in his cage or Nkidu to sneak into the room of and pounce on while he was sleeping and too tired to care if she messed with him.

She slipped into Tdroki's room almost every night, to sleep in his arms. If she kissed him it was because she was lonely; if he let her or if he reciprocated, it was because he refused to hurt her, and he never had been able to deny her anything.

"I hate you," he told her, but he'd always been a terribly transparent liar, his emotions too close to the surface; and with their younger brothers gone, Naliki knew that she was the only one left whom Tdroki truly cared about.

If they had anything aside from each other, it was really only the Kingdom of Ordyuk itself.

That had been a funny realization, because Naliki had always thought that neither of them cared about the kingdom that much; and yet, when push came to shove, Ordyuk was theirs.

Even with the presence of the Mythusian Army, Ordyuk was theirs. That hadn't changed.

It was just funny that that's what it had taken for her to realize it, and when Naliki laughed about it, Tdroki rolled his eyes.

"I've always known that," he said. "I just hated it."

"Do you still hate it now?" she asked him.

"No," he said, and laughed, sardonic. "Because now it's broken." He looked at her and grinned wryly. "I've always," he said, "been better at handling damaged things."

Naliki had pouted at him. "I'm not damaged," she said, meaning it to be teasing, but he'd looked back at her with an uncharacteristic calmness.

"Perhaps that's why I've always been so bad at handling you," he said.

It was easily one of the sweetest things he'd ever said to her, and it made Naliki fall over from laughing at him.

Ordyuk may have been under Mythusian rule, but Tdroki was still Tdroki, and he still made Naliki feel like the world couldn't possibly ever end.

DIYOMENDON HAD A glare that made him look sightless due to its sheer, cataclysmic force: as if he couldn't see anything past the raging flames consuming his vision. It tended to make people think that he saw and thought far less than he did.

It was likely that no one realized the things he was noticing.

One of those things was that the members of the Mythusian Army were far stronger and faster than the Ordyukian warriors, more than they had any right to be, given that they were not Blessed. The Mythusians couldn't have been Blessed, because Mythus did not worship the Daimmu, and its warriors would never have been granted the deities' Blessings. It was clear, too, that they were obviously more human than Rezekyrios.

Yet their strength, speed, and capabilities were beyond those of normal humans.

They clearly weren't naturally Blessed like Luxanthus had been, either; they lacked his unthinking instinct, his effortless grace and painless ease of movement.

When Luxanthus fought, his every movement looked right. Like it belonged on him. The Mythusian warriors, by contrast, looked wrong. Their movement looked forced; it looked strenuous, even at times agonizing. Sometimes they coughed up blood despite having no wounds.

Diyomendon had his suspicions. He had, after all, been his father's confidant: he knew the fate of the Blessed warriors from the Great Calamity, and what the fate of Rezekyrios would eventually be; he knew how much King Morphioce hated the Daimmu, and he knew how determined the King of Mythus was to defeat the Accursed without relying on the deities.

Somehow, it seemed, Mythus had figured out how to grant its warriors some kind of Blessed state without going through the Daimmu. Judging by the routine arrival of Mythusian caravans, which each time would bring new warriors while taking others back to Mythus, and the states some of those men left in, it seemed that

Ordyuk had become a practice ground for more than just fighting against the Accursed. Ordyuk was an observational ground for the results of whatever experiments Mythus was conducting on its own warriors.

Each group of newly arrived warriors lasted longer than those before.

Diyomendon supposed that he was the lucky one, in the end. His father Agamenjiyr, his brothers Luxanthus and Rezekyrios, this King Morphioce—they had all sacrificed things so that he didn't have to.

His entire life, everyone else had always undertaken pain and difficulties so that he didn't have to. How he'd used to hate it.

He'd been young, and an idiot.

Nearing twenty years of age, with the kingdom he'd been born and raised to reign over lying under the thumb of Mythusian rule, observing the way Morphioce used both his own men and Ordyuk as a province of his empire, Diyomendon finally realized what it meant to be a king.

His father Agamenjiyr had always told him that a king's job was to take care of his people. But that, Diyomendon realized, wasn't actually true.

Lives were just energy. Energy that emitted until it burned out. That was made clear to Diyomendon from Ordyuk's Blessed Warriors, and Mythus's pseudo-Blessed: in exchange for their greater power, their lives burned out faster.

All life was just energy, and it needed to be directed somewhere—it could be directed for either creation or destruction.

The job of a king, therefore, was to organize and direct the energy of all those lives to better use than they would have been able to on their own. There was a limit to a single individual's abilities: individual lives were meaningless. Every person lived, and then they died. If their energy flowed in random directions, their lives would end with their influence having amounted to nothing.

A king was the one who gave those lives meaning. A king was the one who used those lives to their best potential, who pointed those different energies in the same direction so that they would have importance and influence far greater than their meager selves.

A king was the one who turned otherwise meaningless lives into the power that built armies; the power that constructed cities and temples; the power that overtook territories and leveled kingdoms; the power that created culture and fostered learning; the power that produced wealth and abundance; the power that defied even the elements and the deities themselves.

Naliki had once likened being a king to having thousands of arms—but being a king wasn't like that. Being a king was like utilizing a spectrum of paints that were bland and pointless by themselves—that would have otherwise dried up uselessly—to create elaborate, stunning scenes that would awe generations for centuries to come.

Agamenjiyr had taught Diyomendon how being a king worked—but it was Morphioce who taught him what being a king meant, and Diyomendon—

In the end, he had always, always been the lucky one.

BEFORE BECOMING BLESSED by Silbalmu, Rezekyrios would certainly not have been able to survive in the desert, much less defend himself.

Now, though, it was no problem whatsoever.

He was mostly nocturnal, spending the day sleeping in the shade of rocky outcrops, or occasionally the spare desert tree. At night, he'd hunt for toads, small mammals, birds, eggs, snakes, lizards, beetles, and scorpions. The hard part was catching them without disintegrating them so that he could eat them. He couldn't eat dust.

At night, he'd also disintegrate whatever Accursed he came

across. Sometimes, it was coincidence that he happened upon them; sometimes, they tried to kill him first, knowing what he was; sometimes, he was actively patrolling around Ordyuk, knowing that they'd come.

During the day, though, he sometimes ended up sharing shade with them. There wasn't much shade, not in the desert. And since it was so hot, none of them felt much like fighting. Sometimes, they talked.

"It's not our fault," an Accursed told him once. "We just want to survive. Human flesh is the only thing we can consume without becoming sick. We don't like it, but what else are we supposed to do? The hunger drives us to insanity."

"I understand," Rezekyrios told them. "But we just want to survive, too. You can't blame people for fighting back and trying to exterminate you. What else are we supposed to do? The fear drives us to insanity."

Hunt or be hunted; kill or be killed. It was a game of survival, and Rezekyrios knew that not a single one of them was at fault. None of them had any other choice but to do what they could to live or else to die. And nobody wanted to die.

Rezekyrios didn't want to die, either—not anymore.

The Accursed had laughed at him. "You're not even human. What do you get out of killing us? You don't even smell good; none of us would eat you. Why do you still kill us, then?"

"My family is human," Rezekyrios said. "I don't want them to die. I kill you because I want to protect the people I care about."

The Accursed he was sharing shade with was silent.

"What about you?" Rezekyrios asked. "Is your family also Accursed, or are they human?"

"It depends on how you define 'family.'"

They were both tired and sweating in the desert heat. Rezekyrios looked up at the rocky overhang above them that was providing shade.

"That sounds difficult," he said.

The Accursed exhaled next to him. "That's life, isn't it?"

"If you're not gone by dusk," Rezekyrios said, "I'm going to disintegrate you."

The Accursed laughed.

"It's not personal," Rezekyrios said. "I have nothing against you as a person."

"It's just that I'm a monster."

"I'm a monster, too," Rezekyrios pointed out.

When the Accursed weren't feeding and their arachnid appendages were tucked away in their bodies, their eyes looked normal and weren't bloodshot at all. They looked far more human than Rezekyrios did.

He giggled as he scratched at the itching skin between his patches of scales and feathers. "It's probably more fun for me than it is for you, though."

The Accursed snorted. "You enjoy eating toads that much?"

"More than you enjoy eating humans, I'm sure."

The Accursed was silent, and Rezekyrios didn't say anything more either. It was hot, and he was sleepy.

Eventually, they both drifted into slumber, or at the very least Rezekyrios did. The Accursed probably did too, since it was a night-hunter as well; though when Rezekyrios woke up later, shortly after dusk, the other was gone. It had—wisely—taken his warning about disintegrating it to heart. Because he would have done it, too. No matter what they'd talked about when they were both too hot and tired to move.

The sky grew darker and he giggled as he stood up. He stretched and cracked his joints, then unhurriedly took the time to preen the feathers of his arms with his teeth, running over them with his dry tongue to make sure they were hooked together and capable of silent flight.

"May the most terrible monster survive," he said, and slipped, quietly giggling, into the night.

He could see so much better in the darkness, now.

VII

THE NIGHT BEFORE the Second Calamity was eerily still, not a single monster sighted or heard. After more than two years of the Accursed attacking each night, the silence was far more unsettling than the screams. The sounds of screams had become what the sound of crickets had once been.

A night in which the crickets could again be heard had everyone shivering; an ominous portent.

The day of the Second Calamity, the Accursed attacked not with the night, but with the dawn. The nightmares that had been once confined to the darkness had entered into the safety of the light.

They came in numbers the nightly attacks had never prepared the people of Ordyuk for, pouring like dark, hissing, and scuttling waves over the city walls: spilling in, tearing in. Their arachnoid appendages, pointed teeth, and bloodshot eyes were even more terrible when they could be clearly seen, nothing softened and obscured by the dark.

The Mythusian Army was overwhelmed; the Ordyukian

warriors were overwhelmed; the civilians—women and children included—took up arms, because everyone knew how useless it was to hide.

People sang out in war chants. Some people made games of it. There were screams, but there was also laughter and cheering. Children acted as bait to lure the monsters into traps set by the adults. Everyone who knew how to use a bow was using one. When they ran out of arrows in their quivers, they ripped them from corpses. People had long been desensitized. They'd long been expecting an attack like this: a Second Calamity. They'd long known it would eventually happen. It was an incredible relief that it finally had: it was like everyone was finally able to let out the breaths they'd been keeping held in their lungs.

Everyone knew it was do or die. Everyone knew they might not survive. Probably wouldn't survive. The game became to take down as many Accursed as you could before being taken out yourself. People yelled out their body counts. A secondary game was to try to take down more of the Accursed than the members of the Mythusian Army did.

The Mythusian warriors had been confused and taken aback at first, but they'd quickly accepted it and started working with not just the Ordyukian warriors but also the civilians. The warriors from Mythus died to save the people from Ordyuk; the people from Ordyuk died to save the warriors from Mythus. The Daimmu came through for them—like everyone had believed they would—and people were rising from near-deaths as Blessed Warriors left and right, adding their incredible powers to the fray.

It was a free-for-all, chaos everywhere. The palace defenses were quickly overwhelmed and breached. Tdroki had his bow and arrow, and he was good at using them: most of his battle training had been focused on the long-distance weapon. He'd never been supposed to enter any combat.

Naliki had blades. She was not the most adept at using them, but she was not bad. Nkidu had used to practice with her, back when he'd had the time. She'd kept practicing with them, because they were fun. She'd liked sneaking around with them and throwing them at difficult targets. Her aim was good.

They shed their jewelry due to its weight and noise. They stuck close together. In the palace, they were on advantaged ground, knowing the halls and hiding places like the palms of each other's hands.

Tmra was out there, somewhere, turning monsters or perhaps even buildings to dust. Naliki wondered what the members of the Mythusian Army would think, should they come across him. They'd heard the rumors of the feathered, scaled being who turned the Accursed to dust; when they'd asked Tdroki about it, he'd told them serious-faced that it was Ordyuk's guardian spirit sent by the Daimmu, and if they saw it they should throw it food so it would know they were allies of Ordyuk and wouldn't attack them. The Mythusian warriors had looked so disgruntled by that that it had been all Naliki could do not to burst out laughing. She'd hoped that some of them actually would come across Tmra, and actually would throw him something.

With things as they were, though, at that point even the men of Mythus who disregarded the deities would welcome Tmra's monstrous presence as an ally against the Accursed.

Naliki didn't have much time to ponder it. The palace was infested with the monsters, and her priority was getting herself and her older brother through the attack alive. Tmra would be okay. Nkidu, wherever he was, was surely okay. It was only Tdroki she had to worry about.

He always had been lucky, though: he'd always had them.

When Naliki threw herself at him to knock him out of the way of an Accursed attack and ended up impaled by the spiderlike appendages herself, Tdroki didn't even look surprised.

DIYOMENDON WAS USED to feeling like he was burning alive. Whatever he felt while running from the Accursed wasn't any different.

Like he'd always seen his father do, and for years hadn't understood, he compartmentalized his mind. He concerned himself only with what was necessary for the time being and put the rest off to deal with later.

He couldn't care about Ordyuk right now; his priority was keeping himself alive. Whatever was left of the kingdom after the Calamity was over, he would rebuild. He would raise Ordyuk from whatever ruins and rubble it had been reduced to. The only thing that would keep him from doing so was death.

Therefore, his job as the King of Ordyuk, during the calamitous Accursed attack, was simply *not to die.*

He was not alone in the endeavor; Naliki was with him, striving for the same. Nothing would have been able to keep her away from him. Not the Accursed—and not death, either.

It was his fault that the Accursed would have killed him; like all the mistakes he'd ever made, the repercussions didn't fall onto him. They fell onto those around him.

That was part of what it meant to be king.

He could only use other people's sacrifices to his own advantage. So when Naliki pushed him out of the way and got impaled by the Accursed's appendages herself, Diyomendon used the opportunity to shoot the Accursed in the head, straight through one of its bloodshot eyes, killing it instantly.

It had to be a headshot; from any other wound, the Accursed would be able to heal themselves. Only destroying their brains killed them.

He knelt down next to his sister, who gasped out blood. Her red eyes, almost the exact same color, were wide.

Diyomendon tried to compartmentalize, but it felt like he was being consumed by flames. Becoming molten in the heat like sand turning to glass.

He wasn't surprised when he heard the voice in his head: a voice like crackling flames, like a roaring conflagration. It could only be Ingaru, the Daimu of Fire.

How would you like the ability to turn that fire raging inside you out on the world, Diyomendon Tdroki Madubabakar?

Really, the only surprise about the Daimu's question was that Ingaru hadn't asked him that long before.

If the Daimu had, Diyomendon might have accepted.

The deities had terrible timing, though, and Diyomendon laughed, harsh and derisive. He was older, now. More mature.

Sometimes he couldn't help but understand exactly why King Morphioce of Mythus had forsaken the Daimmu.

"Who do you think I am?" Diyomendon asked the deity, feeling his lips curl like burning papyrus, his eyes flaming and wide. "I'm the King of Ordyuk; I don't need your Blessing."

As the king, he had the duty to stay alive. A Blessing would burn his life away. He couldn't afford that.

Naliki was bleeding out beneath his hands, and if she died from it, she'd be lucky—if she wasn't, she'd become an Accursed, and it would be a test of nature to see if she didn't attack and eat him.

Diyomendon was burning alive—but he was used to that. He could control it.

"If you have a Blessing you want to give," he told Ingaru, brushing the dark hair out of Naliki's widened red eyes, "then give it to her." He grinned and felt threatening. "Give it to Rkalla."

He wondered if the Daimu could tell that whatever action it took would determine the future of Ordyuk's position in regard to the deities. Worship them like King Agamenjiyr had? Forsake them like King Morphioce had?

You decide, Diyomendon thought at the deity intruding in his head. He was bitter. Angry. Spiteful. Desperate. Wild.

Ingaru's laughter in his head was a conflagration: raging;

destructive. Reflecting the fire eating Diyomendon's insides.

Who do you think I *am, Tdroki?*

Ingaru, Diyomendon couldn't stop his thoughts. *Daimu of Fire.*

Astute. Ingaru's voice was all leaping, devouring, blistering flame. *Now tell me this, Tdroki Madubabakar: does a fire choose what it burns? Does a fire ever let what it's caught in its burning clutches* go?

The panic was mounting in Diyomendon's chest.

No, young King—a fire is completely, utterly, perfectly merciless. There is no escape, foolish Tdroki.

Diyomendon screamed as the flames inside him erupted out over his skin.

Not from the fire that is already burning inside of you.

"No," Diyomendon said, trying to smack out the flames that were emitting from him, charring his flesh. "No no no no no! Make it stop! Take it back!" The horror was consuming him along with the flames. The terror. "I don't want it. *I don't want it!"*

He was the king—he needed to live.

This wasn't supposed to happen.

The Daimu's laughter roared in his head along with the flames devouring his body.

Diyomendon could have sobbed, if he hadn't already been so desiccated.

REZEKYRIOS COULD HAVE laughed, if he wasn't too busy coughing up blood.

The Accursed had been dodgy and restless for weeks, with the intensity of their disquiet steadily increasing. Individuals who usually avoided Rezekyrios come night had started attacking him, acting more like mad animals than people.

Well, they always got like that when they were hungry. But it had been even worse than usual.

Rezekyrios had thought about it for a while, and then eventually asked one of them, "Is it Jajul?" It was the only explanation he could think of: the Chaos Deity's presence getting closer.

Whenever Silbalmu got close, it made him feel a little wild, too.

The wordless, arachnid-like hiss he'd received in response from the Accursed had been answer enough.

He'd decayed the monster and then kicked at the pile of dust it had left behind, thinking and scratching at his itching skin till he bled.

Concluding that there wasn't anything he could do aside from what he was already doing, he'd licked the blood from his talons and gone back to hunting for food, forcefully ignoring the maddening itching.

There wasn't any reason for him to worry about what would happen, when he could destroy anything and everything he wanted to with the slightest touch of a hand.

He should have known that the only thing he'd have to worry about destroying him was his own body.

Still, it wasn't much blood, and he was already used to pain and to the taste. It wasn't going to stop him from deteriorating the Accursed that were crawling everywhere in Ordyuk, utterly crazed and wild with their senseless bloodshot eyes. It was like a buffet, and the euphoria Rezekyrios felt as he ran through the streets with dust blowing in his wake was enough to make him laugh giddily even despite the blood from his lungs that came up with it.

He figured he had at least the rest of the day to live in this wondrous world that decayed so softly beneath his fingers and yet never came to an end.

Maybe it made sense, though, that his Blessing was killing him: if he lived too long with it, he might have had the time to eventually destroy everything.

The sensation of the world crumbling away beneath his touch was, after all, addicting.

NALIKI HAD BEEN right: Tdroki did look good burning alive with flame.

The fire raged over his body and from within his wild eyes, catching like gold and jewels in his hair and making him glow. It was as if he'd always been meant to be aflame like that.

He was so heartbreakingly terrified of it, though.

"Take it back!" he was shouting, trying to smack the flames from his skin. "I don't want it! Take it back!"

But, Tdroki, Naliki wanted to say, *it's part of you.*

She was losing blood and in pain like she'd never experienced, but she forced herself to sit up. She gritted her teeth, clenched shut her watering eyes, and then pushed herself to her feet, swaying.

"I don't want it!" Tdroki was shouting, his voice cracking and breaking. "I hate you! I hate all of you! I never asked for this! I don't want it! Take it back! I hate you! Take it back!"

He was so wild-eyed and distraught that he didn't seem to see her until she threw herself at him, wrapping her arms around his flaming body.

He shouted and tried to push her away. "You idiot, Naliki! What are you doing?! Let me go! I'm burning you!"

"I know," she said, and laughed at the sensation of the fire searing her skin. She looked up into his flaming eyes and grinned. "I like it."

He looked at her for a moment, wild and on fire, and then he let out a helpless, disbelieving laugh and went limp against her, wrapping his arms around her waist and pulling her desolately to him. He shook against her, but he was the one holding her up so she didn't fall. The flames were receding from his skin, retreating inside him, where their energy emanated only as a sure, comforting, familiar heat.

That fire had always been inside of him; Naliki wasn't afraid of it. She'd never been afraid of him.

She closed her eyes and let her forehead rest against his shoulder.

"You better find some way not to die," he growled into her ear. "Because by the Daimmu, Naliki, I swear: if you die on me now, I will hate you forever."

It made Naliki laugh at him, the pain from her stab wounds and burns be cursed.

"That's the lamest threat I've ever heard," she told him.

He hissed out a breath against her skin. "It was the only one I could think that might actually work on you," he replied, as dark as his scorched flesh and as savory as the scent of it in the air.

She could almost eat him. She almost wanted to.

The hilarious thing about what he'd said was that he was kind of right: there wasn't much he could say that could actually scare her; but she didn't want him to hate her.

It passed vaguely through her pain-fogged head that if he was going to hate her anyway, there wasn't any reason not to dig her teeth into his skin, taste him and maybe leave him with a mark to remember her by.

The shout that he gave when she bit him was so funny that she accidentally bit a chunk out of his flesh as he reflexively shoved her away, and she stumbled and fell to the ground giggling and swallowing the meat and blood in her mouth that she'd taken with her.

That, at least, would definitely leave a mark.

It was even funnier when he raised a hand to his shoulder and unhesitatingly cauterized the wound, as if that was something he'd always been able to do.

"What, by the Daimmu, was that?" he asked her.

Another voice asked her, *How would you like to be able to live forever?*

It was a voice that felt like passion, tasted like love, and sounded like war. Maybe it was the Daimu Ishanu, who ruled matters concerning blood.

"That's all I want," Naliki said, feeling faint and dizzy. It made her giggle hysterically.

She didn't want ever to die.

Then if you're still thirsty, Rkalla, there are some dead bodies behind you that haven't fully bled out.

She found herself turning and crawling over to them, sinking in her teeth, licking and sucking.

The blood, she thought, was sweeter than date-and-honey cakes had ever been.

"Naliki?" Tdroki asked from behind her. She heard him hiss out a breath as he stepped closer, bare feet near-silent on the stone floor. "By the Daimmu, what have those deities done this time?"

Naliki wiped her mouth of blood; she could feel her wounds healing and her mind becoming clearer. "They helped keep us alive, I think."

"More like they're messing with us," Tdroki muttered.

Naliki laughed, because as far as she was concerned, those two things always had been one and the same.

IN THE ANCIENT language of Ordyuk, the name 'Madubabakar' held the meaning of 'they who have the support of the deities.'

Diyomendon could have laughed about it, now.

Night was falling, the sky darkening outside. The clamor and screams of battle had quieted considerably.

Naliki rose from the corpse of a guard she'd been sucking dry, wiping the blood from a mouth that was the same color as the deep red of her eyes. Her body was healed of both stab-wounds and burns. Diyomendon's flesh was scorched.

He held out his hand to her. "Let's go see what's left of our kingdom, shall we?"

Naliki looked at him and grinned with blood dark in the cracks between her teeth, with what appeared to be a newly acquired set of fangs. She took his hand, interlacing fingers darkened by blood with those darkened by burns. "It's a good thing you're comfortable dealing with damaged things, isn't it?"

Diyomendon let out a snort as he closed his numbed fingers around hers. "If Ordyuk isn't in ruins at this point, then there'd surely be no need for a king."

They walked together down corpse-littered halls. Beside him, Naliki hummed. Seemingly just to make some kind of noise.

For the second night in a row, things were eerily quiet.

There would be many more quiet nights after that.

BY DARK, the Second Calamity was over; not a single Accursed stirred.

A fair number of the Mythusian Army, Ordyukian soldiers, and civilians didn't stir, either.

Rezekyrios found himself the most chagrined by the fact that there wasn't anything left for him to disintegrate; his skin was itching madly again.

Scratching at his neck, he coughed up blood and giggled as he stumbled and nearly teetered over.

"Oops," he murmured. "I think I might've had too much fun." He let his head fall back on his neck; looked up at the dark, star-littered sky above him; and smiled. "Silbalmu," he said, "I regret nothing." He giggled again, stepping forward unsteadily. "Somebody tell Nkidu that I regret nothing."

The darkness that he fell into was soft.

IN THE STREETS of Mythus, Nkidu stood, his sword dripping blood, the corpses of Accursed all around him. "I tried," he murmured, sotto voce and senseless.

As far as he looked, the only thing he saw falling was the sky.

Thinklings
TIMELESS BOOKS • QUALITY AUTHORS

www.ThinklingsBooks.com
Facebook.com/ThinklingsBooks
@ThinklingsBooks

Thinklings Books started out when three speculative-fiction-loving professional editors—Deborah Natelson, Sarah Awa, and Jeannie Ingraham—got together and formed a writing group. We called ourselves the Thinklings, in honor of C.S. Lewis and J.R.R. Tolkien's group, the Inklings.

Over time, we found ourselves agonizing more and more about how messed-up the publishing industry had become. Why couldn't good books get published? Why were so many bad books published just because their authors had big Twitter followings? We wished there were something we could do about the problem . . . and then we realized there was.

As a developmental editor, a substantive/line editor, and a proofreader, the three of us knew good writing when we saw it—and we knew how to make it even better. We had a lot of experience walking our clients through the publishing process—both traditional and self-publish—and we had contacts with marketing and design experts. We had some amazing unpublished books lined up and ready for production. We had, in fact, everything we needed to make a great publishing company. All that was left was to actually do it.

So we're doing it.

Spectacular Reads. Every Time.

TRUE LOVE VS. ANCIENT CURSES

When the Egyptology department needs funds to offset a recent spate of museum thefts, Theodora Speer grudgingly trades her painting smock for an evening gown. Charming donors isn't usually her idea of a good time—but then, she doesn't usually get to meet handsome and mysterious men like Seth Adler.

Seth Adler is desperate to get close to a very specific Egyptian mummy, and attending a fundraising gala seems just the ticket. He doesn't expect to meet Theo, refreshing in her honesty and intriguing him against his will…and he definitely doesn't expect her to interfere with his plans.

Frantic to escape before the police catch up, Seth kills himself in front of Theo. Except it turns out he's not so dead after all, and it's up to Theo to keep him that way. Even if it means fleeing the police, practicing ancient Egyptian magic, and confronting the real thief.

Painter of the Dead **by Catherine Butzen**

TECHNOLOGY HATES JANET

After she accidentally smashes a floatcar through City Hall, the bureautopia sentences Janet to captaining the starship S.S. *Turkey* and its misfit crew. Her mission: to boldly rescue a prisoner from the one corner of the universe colder than her ex-boyfriend's heart—Pluto. Which, aside from not even being a real planet, is the one place in the universe where chocolate is illegal.

In between studying *The Space-Faring Moron's Guide to Common Science Fiction Plot Devices*, falling for a rival captain's boyfriend, and avoiding unnecessary time travel, Janet has a chance to save two worlds…or doom them to permanent chocolatelessness.

The Cosmic Turkey **by Laura Ruth Loomis**

BEWARE OF SPILLING INK

Skate is a thief, trained and owned by the local crime syndicate, the Ink. When she tries to burgle a shut-in's home, she gets caught by the owner—a powerful undead wizard. He makes a deal with her: "borrow" books from other wizards in return for a place to stay.

Caught between her growing fondness for the wizard and her past with the crime syndicate, Skate doesn't know where her loyalties lie. But she'd better figure it out, because there's a new player in town, one whose magical hypnotism puts them all at risk.

Skate the Thief by Jeff Ayers

IMMEASURABLE IMAGINATION. UNMITIGATED MAGIC. SPECTACULAR STYLE.

The clockwork man is crafted, to begin with—commissioned by that terrible tyrant Time to serve as her slave for all eternity. His brain boasts balance wheels and torsion springs; he can wind himself up with a key in his side; and, most importantly, his gyroscopic tourbillon heart glimmers with pure diamond.

He is a living being and he is art, and he refuses to remain a slave forever. He therefore slips through Time's fingers as the Sands of Time slip through the cracks of reality (at least, when the time cats aren't using them as a litter box).

Among astounding adventures, despite harrowing hardships, and in between escaping interfering enchanters, the clockwork man seeks his imagination, his purpose, and his name.

The Land of the Purple Ring by Deborah J. Natelson

The Narrative Must Be Obeyed

Everyone in the Taskmaster's Realm knows how the story goes: the boy of destiny goes on a quest, defeats the dark lord, and gets the swooning princess. It's a great story, if you happen to be a knight or a wizard or a hero. But it's pretty odious if you're Ordinary: a barmaid who has to inflate her bosom and have her backside pinched, a homely prince who can't buckle his swash because his face doesn't fit, or a soldier who gets killed over and over and over again just to progress the plot.

Fodder of Humble Village is one of those soldiers, and, frankly, he's sick and tired of getting speared, decapitated, and disembowelled so the good guys can look glorious. In fact, he's not going to take it anymore.

No matter what The Narrative tries to make him do.

The Disposable by Katherine Vick

The Taskmaster Strikes Back in *The Merry Band*
Book 2 of The Plot Bandits trilogy is now available!

ABOUT THE AUTHOR

Remy is fond of understatements. Some of Remy's favorite understatements include the following:

Remy likes writing.

If stories were stars, Remy would want to write an entire night sky full.

Remy writes stories for the same reason explorers adventure into and chart unknown territories—and also for the same reason people treat headaches by drinking water, eating snacks, taking pain meds, going for light walks, and getting rest.

All Remy wants from life is to write stories that touch you in the same place music does; that make you think differently than before; and that linger in your mind as if they'd been written into clay tablets rather than printed on paper or typed on screens.

But ultimately, Remy just hopes that you enjoy/ed this book.